OPERATION LIG

Carol Sinclair was .... small town near Wellington, New Zeal....... ....est of four children. From an early age s.. would invent stories to entertain her siblings and friends and after leaving school went on to do a variety of jobs involving writing. Her inspiration for *Operation Lighthouse* came from her sadness about endangered species. She says, "Conservation often seems more of a dreary duty than a fight for the planet. I wanted to create a world where the idea of saving the environment could be exciting." Carol has written several books, although *Operation Lighthouse* is her first title for children. She lives in Wiltshire with her husband, the artist Ray Ching.

OPERATION LIGHTHOUSE

CAROL SINCLAIR

WALKER BOOKS
AND SUBSIDIARIES
LONDON • BOSTON • SYDNEY

*The characters and events described in this book
are fictional. Although many conservation organizations
are working in various ways throughout the world to
monitor and prevent trade in endangered species,
no similarity to any particular organization is intended.*

The author and publisher are grateful for kind permission from the
Literary Trustees of Walter de la Mare, and the Society of Authors
as their representative, to quote from his poem "The Listeners".

The quotation from "Jim who ran away from his nurse, and
was eaten by a lion" is reprinted by permission of PFD on behalf of
The Estate of Hilaire Belloc. © as printed in the original volume.

First published 2002 by Walker Books Ltd
87 Vauxhall Walk, London SE11 5HJ

2 4 6 8 10 9 7 5 3

Text © 2002 Carol Sinclair
Cover illustration © 2002 Mark Preston

This book has been typeset in Sabon

Printed and bound in Great Britain
by J.H. Haynes and Co. Ltd.

British Library Cataloguing in Publication Data:
a catalogue record for this book is
available from the British Library

ISBN 0-7445-5988-X

To Leon, Alexander and Lily-Carol

CHAPTER ONE

I'll remember that day for the rest of my life.

At first I blamed Tommo, but then I realized it was even worse for him than me. The trouble is, he always fools around and acts crazy on the viewing platform, and it's so high – he really worries me.

That day, as usual, he was carrying on, leaping about, pretending to be Superman or Arnold Schwarzenegger or someone. I wasn't taking much notice because I was worried about the storm. I could see it coming over the sea, a sort of shower curtain hanging from the sky, grey and ominous ... a sinister manifestation of the force of nature (I read that in a book). It was just a patch of rain but it was beating so hard on the sea that it flattened the waves underneath it as it moved slowly towards us.

It's amazing what you can see from the top

of a lighthouse. You'd think it would be all just empty sea, apart from when ships go past. But there are weird things out there just under the surface, things that make all sorts of sudden swirls and waves in the ocean, even on calm days. Dad says they're hidden rocks, but I reckon I've seen strange animals – maybe even sea-serpents and prehistoric monsters.

Sometimes we see tornadoes: long, thin tunnels of wind that swivel over the sea, sucking up water and stuff. And whole schools of whales taking their babies to feeding grounds thousands of miles away, diving and then coming to the surface, all spouting water like fountains. And hundreds of porpoises swimming together, chasing their food, rolling and tumbling over each other, showing their dark blue backs and their silver tummies and leaping high out of the water as if they're playing leap-frog. And seals giving their babies swimming lessons. At the beginning the babies are so funny – they splash and splutter and try to stand on their heads in the water, waving their hind-flippers in the air. But before long they're swimming in deep water and riding on the tops of the big waves, all by themselves. It's never boring, looking out to sea.

But that day, watching the storm, I was in a kind of frozen state – like a rabbit terrified by a snake. I was really scared, but I couldn't get my act together to run inside. Tommo – his name's really Thomas – was leaping around like crazy. The storm had gone to his head – probably the positive ions in the air. Do you know about them? They make people sort of weird when a storm is on the way.

"I'm going to wait until it nearly hits and then fly for safety!" he yelled, his hair blowing all over his face. Squawkette, our parrot, clung to his shoulder, bobbing up and down with excitement, screeching "Faster than speeding bullets! Faster than speeding bullets!"

For a moment I looked down at the sea, crashing and beating itself against the rocks. Every now and then white waves flung themselves up the lighthouse walls, as if they were trying to suck us down into the depths.

Everything on the island was thrashing about in the wind. The grass around the base of the lighthouse was rippling and flattening on the ground as if hordes of invisible feet were trampling it down. The forest trees down the side of the valley were tossing from side to side. Suddenly a flash of lightning lit up the old ruin in the distance, making it look just like Dracula's castle.

"Hey – did you see that?" Thomas ran to the other side, nearly tripping over Betty, our cat, who was in a state! She followed Thomas, nagging and complaining in her funny, gruff voice, then jumped up and nipped his fingers. She was warning him, and he knew it, but he flipped his hand in front of her face.

"Oh, shut up, Betty!" He was irritated. "Nothing can phase the man of steel!" he yelled in a silly, superhero voice.

The rain was now only a few metres from the lighthouse. I'd had enough. "Come on, Tommo, stop messing about. It's too windy! I'm off inside." I shouted, but the wind whipped the words right out of my mouth. I didn't even know whether he had heard me.

I picked up Betty, made a dash for the doorway and turned to see Thomas leap towards me. But suddenly a monster gust of rain and wind slashed, and a mad whirl of red, yellow and blue spun from Thomas's shoulder. Squawkette was snatched away with one ghastly, terrified squawk – and was gone!

Thomas yelled and clutched at the air. I screamed and ran outside again, still hugging Betty, who screeched and clawed at me, struggling to get away.

Squawkette was gone. Definitely gone.

We were stunned. We just stood there with the rain beating down. We couldn't think what to do. For a moment Thomas thought he heard another faint squawk and dashed to the rail, peering into the storm – but nothing. I ran to the other side, screaming, "Squawkette – Squawkette!"

Thomas ran around, peering over the railing, shouting her name. But there was no sight or sound of her. Betty was wriggling madly, so I ran back inside.

"I'm going for help!" I yelled – although what help, I had no idea. I ran downstairs, shrieking, "Mum! Mum!" Betty jumped out of my arms and ran ahead, calling, "Airk, airk, airk", loudly.

Mum heard the commotion and came running up.

"What's the matter, Betty?" She picked her up and then dropped her again quickly as she felt the wet fur. "Whatever is going on?" she asked as we came clattering down the stairs, soaked to our skins. She saw we were frantic. "What's happened? Tell me – what's happened?" she asked, putting her arms round me as I burst into tears.

All I could say was "Squawkette... Squawkette... Squawk— Squawk—"

"Squawkette is gone!" Thomas burst out, and he sank down on the stairs and buried his head in his arms. Betty stood up on her hind legs and tried to burrow her face into him, giving gentle little miaows. She hates to see us upset.

"How?" Mum sat down too, pulling me down beside her. I was crying loudly. "Shhh, Polly. How did it happen, Thomas?"

"Thomas wouldn't come inside when I told him – Betty was nagging and nagging – he wouldn't take any notice—" I burst out.

"Shut up!" Thomas glared at me and then buried his face in Betty's fur.

"Shhh, Polly." Mum put her other arm around Thomas and patted his shoulder. "Just tell me quietly and calmly what happened."

Thomas told the story, with a lot of sniffing, and I didn't interrupt. No one loved Squawkette better than Thomas and no one would suffer more now that she was gone.

"Oh ... oh! How terrible," said Mum when he had finished. She thought for a minute and then said, slowly, "I suppose it's just possible – faintly possible – that some ship somewhere might pick her up..." She frowned, biting her lip, and then shook her head. "Maybe I'm just being silly."

Thomas jumped up. "We'll ask Dad to put out a message – over the satellite. Someone might see her, they *might*..." And he was gone, shouting to Dad with Betty running after him. Mum and I followed more slowly. I didn't really think there was a chance, but maybe...?

In the communications room, Dad was sitting in front of banks of monitors, computer keyboards, knobs, dials and levers. He was staring into the radar screen, watching the beam sweeping around the green circular map. The calmness of the room and the familiar *blip, blip* of the beam were so comforting after the chaos of the storm that for a moment no one broke the silence.

We knew we shouldn't interrupt Dad – human lives could depend on what was happening on the screen. He was teaching us to operate all the equipment and we knew he needed to really concentrate to interpret the signals. The screen was filled with a mass of what was called "sea clutter" and "rain clutter", caused by the radar echoes contacting the stormy waves and heavy rain. Dad was having trouble interpreting the picture.

"What d'you want, Thomas? I'm very busy at the moment," he said gruffly, tweaking the sea clutter control.

Thomas turned away and I could see he was giving up. The possibility of saving one small parrot in the storm outside was not on. Ships of all sizes would be in trouble out there right now. Squawkette was probably already dead. It was useless – a waste of time. Thomas sniffled and started to walk out of the room, but Mum broke in quickly.

"Dylan, Squawkette has been blown away in the storm. Can't we do something?"

Dad's head shot round. "When?" he demanded.

"A few minutes ago – blown off my shoulder in a big gust of wind," Thomas began.

"She was just snatched away – there was nothing we could do – it was terrible," I said.

"Dad – please, please do something!" begged Thomas.

Dad looked at us, shaking his head. "Look at the radar screen," he said. "There won't be a chance."

But we didn't want to know that. "Please, please, Daddy – just try!"

"We can't give up yet!"

"We can't give up till we've tried everything…"

We were begging for a miracle which, in our heart of hearts, we knew would never happen.

"I'll send out a radio message to all ships in the vicinity," said Dad reluctantly. "But it won't do any good. Anyone out there today will be too busy saving his own skin to bother about a wind-blown parrot."

Betty ran over to him and stood on her hind legs, her front paws on his knee and her little face looking up at him.

"Angow," she miaowed, as if she were saying "thank you".

CHAPTER TWO

After that we didn't feel like doing much.
Mum told us to change out of our wet clothes
and then we slouched down to the kitchen. She
was just taking a batch of chocolate chip cookies out of the Aga, and while they cooled she
made us hot chocolate. We drank it slowly.
Neither of us could say a word. Mum handed
us a plate of cookies, still warm, but I felt too
bad to eat more than a bite.

"We should be eating something really horrible – castor oil, or bread and water – as a
punishment," I mumbled.

"Don't be silly," said Mum gently. "You
need the energy. Anyway, how do you know
about castor oil?"

"I read it in a book," I said, hardly daring
to look at Thomas. I knew he was trying not
to cry.

Mum moved very quietly as she rinsed

things and stacked the dishwasher. Then she came and sat down at the table, her hands wrapped around a cup of coffee.

"You know, animals don't think about dying," she said. "They just fight on. Squawkette will be too busy battling with the winds – she won't be aware of disaster. She may even be enjoying herself!"

We looked at her glumly. We knew she was only trying to cheer us up, but it didn't work. Thomas put his head on the table.

"I can't believe it. I can't believe it," he said after a while. "I just can't believe I was so stupid!" He covered his head with his arm.

"Well," said Mum, trying to sound cheerful. "She is a bird, after all. Perhaps she'll cope better than we think. Sea birds manage to weather storms. Perhaps she'll find somewhere to shelter and come back when it's over – who knows?"

Thomas lifted his head slightly and looked at her cynically with one eye. "Pigs might fly," he muttered.

"She can fly better than a pig!" said Mum tartly. "Don't give up yet, Thomas."

"Perhaps she's been blown back to the island," I said, trying to cheer him up. "She might be sheltering somewhere right now – somewhere quite close."

"One thing is certain, if she's anywhere nearby, she'll be back as soon as the weather is calmer." Mum used her "there-there-it'll-be-all-right" voice, but we didn't believe her.

"I'm going upstairs," said Thomas moodily, pushing out his chair and shuffling off.

I suddenly felt very tired. "Me too," I said, following him.

Our bedroom was the whole fourth floor, which could be divided into two rooms by a sliding wall. Betty's basket was on my side of the room and Squawkette's perch on Tommo's.

We'd painted the room to look like a clearing in a rainforest. It had taken months – Mum had helped. We'd painted trees, vines and flowers up the walls and then the animals: monkeys swinging from branches, parrots and toucans perching and flying, snakes hanging from trees or crawling out from under logs. Tropical orchids with butterflies on their petals bloomed near the floor. Moss dripped from branches and strange mushrooms peeped out from between gnarled tree roots.

Tarzan ropes hung from the ceiling over each bed and over the doorways. Usually we swung onto our beds, but today we ignored the ropes and flung ourselves down in silence. For a long time nothing was heard, except waves crashing and rain lashing against the windows and an occasional clap of thunder. Every now and then a flash of lightning lit up the walls and the painted animals seemed to flicker with life.

"Remember how she looked when we found her?" I said after a while. Thomas nodded. I could see he didn't want to speak in case he cried again. "Wrapped in paper and squashed into that suitcase with all the other baby macaws?"

"Mmm," Thomas murmured, and then he swallowed hard and in a thick voice he added, "Rebember her little face ... with her terrified eyes ... and that little squawk as we obened the lid?"

The thought of it made me want to cry again. I sniffed loudly, groped under my pillow for a tissue and blew my nose hard.

"Tommo," I mumbled through the tissue, "She survived all that." I crumpled the tissue into a ball and threw it into the wastepaper basket. "Being stuffed into that suitcase by the smugglers – taken onto the plane – the explosion in the air – bobbing for hours in the sea until she floated to our beach. Maybe she *will* survive the storm." Thomas was lying on his back, gazing at the ceiling. I could see he wasn't convinced. He said nothing. "She might, Tommo – she might." My voice sounded unconvincing even to me.

Thomas rolled over with his back to me. "I don't want to talk about it," he said. Then he got up, gave me a tragic look and slid the wall across. And that was that.

I lay looking at the wall, knowing it was no

use saying anything. I didn't feel like saying anything, anyway. I'd never felt so down in my whole life. You see, Squawkette had been more than a pet – she was a kind of symbol of survival against the odds. She kept us believing that a few determined people could win against the masses of organized crime.

Dad knew her history the moment he saw her. His job is to help catch wildlife smugglers, and he knows all about the thousands and thousands of birds and monkeys and other animals that are taken illegally every year from the rainforests by cruel people who only care about making money.

Tommo and I had never been directly involved until one morning when we'd gone down to the beach for a walk and had seen a battered, wet suitcase bobbing on the tide. I yelled to Thomas. It was quite close to the beach and he waded out and pulled it in. We dragged it up the beach, a largish, grey, ordinary-looking suitcase with airline tags on the handle. We could tell it hadn't been long in the sea and it wasn't very heavy, but it was obviously full of something.

I said it was probably just someone's disgusting old holiday clothes, or dirty washing they didn't want to take home, so they'd thrown it overboard from a boat. I was really hoping desperately it would be something exciting, but I always said things like that so I wouldn't feel so disappointed when it turned out to be nothing.

Thomas always thought of the most exciting possibilities and then was usually disappointed. He began trying to force the locks, saying maybe it was bundles of money – like gangsters carry around – thrown overboard in a gangland shooting. The locks were slightly rusty and already becoming crusted up with salt. He got a large stone and began bashing at them until finally one popped and then the other.

I remember he said, "Are you ready, Pol?" and then paused, hands on the lid, eyes wide with excitement, making the moment stretch out for as long as he could, saying maybe it would be the "Genie of the Suitcase" who would grant our every wish … or maybe a stash of stolen treasure or diamonds.

He lifted the lid and the excited expression on his face turned to horror. Dozens and dozens of baby parrots filled the case, all wrapped tightly in paper and stuffed side by side in rows with just their little heads showing, looking like tiny Egyptian mummies. They were all dead except one, who opened its eyes and gave a little squawk for help.

Thomas gasped and his face turned white. He slammed the lid shut, but I grabbed his arm and yelled, "One's still alive – we've got to save it!"

We forced ourselves to open the lid and look at the little bundles again. One blinked its eyes and let out a feeble croak. Slowly, ever so carefully, I eased it out of the suitcase and we rushed back to the lighthouse, yelling for Dad.

He knew exactly what to do. First he mixed up a sort of gunge by chewing up pieces of apple and a banana and spitting it into a cup with the yolk of an egg and a dash of olive oil. Then he stuck it in the blender and poured it into the plastic syringe that Mum used to ice birthday cakes, and gently forcing the bird's beak open he squirted the mixture into its throat. The poor thing swallowed greedily, and after a while Dad unwrapped the small squashed body.

He told us, sadly, that it was a baby female macaw, and that she was very weak. She was so young she hardly had any feathers, just funny little spiky wings. Slowly and painfully she flexed them and squawked again, in a croaky voice. Then she fell over on the table and gazed at us mournfully.

I fell totally in love with her at that moment and begged Dad for us to be able to keep her. Tommo said, Yeah! She could ride on his shoulder, like that pirate who had a parrot – Long John Silver. Dad told us not to get excited – he was sure she wouldn't live.

But she did. Every day we'd rush down to the kitchen and she was still alive, getting stronger and stronger. And so she was ours: Squawkette, named for that tiny squawk she gave when we found her.

Dad told us later that parrots are among the most endangered birds in the world. Soon there may be none left in the wild. Firstly, people cut down the forests they live in, which destroys their homes and their food. And then, poachers take thousands of them from their nests every year, to sell as pets. Many of them die, but the ones that end up in pet shops are really expensive and make huge profits for the smugglers. It's against the law, but people still do it – just for the money. They don't care what happens to the parrots.

Squawkette had been part of an illegal shipment by air from South America. A mysterious explosion had destroyed the plane, and she was probably the only survivor. That's how it had all happened, two years ago. Now we couldn't imagine life without her.

CHAPTER THREE

There was a time when we'd lived in an ordinary sort of house in an ordinary sort of town and had gone to school just like everyone else. We thought it was great.

But one day Dad came home and said we were selling up and all going to live somewhere else. Somewhere very different. We wouldn't be going to school like other kids, although we'd keep on doing lessons. He said he and Mum couldn't tell us where – it was a secret – but that if we didn't like it after two years, we would all come back.

While he was telling us I was looking at Thomas and he was looking at me. I could tell what he was thinking, because I was thinking the same thing. Would we have TV? Would we have computer games? Would we have hamburgers, and pizzas, and bubble-gum … and stuff? Or were they taking us away to an alternative lifestyle?

The first moment we got on our own, we started.

"So!" said Thomas, "Yasmin and Dylan have finally flipped. It's really happened at last!"

We had gone up to his bedroom, supposedly to play a computer game, and I flopped down on the bed and stared at the ceiling. I said gloomily, "They're trying to return to those awful 'good old days' of their childhood, and take us with them."

Thomas groaned. "No electricity – no cars – no junk food. Candles – horse-drawn caravans – lentil stew – all that rubbish they go on and on about." He sat down at the end of the bed and began to bite his nails. "What can we do?" he moaned.

I can't bear the sight of someone biting their nails. "Oh please – Tommo – stop it!" I said.

"OK – OK." He sighed heavily. "What's so wrong with the way we live now, anyway?" he asked. "We *like* computers and cars and skateboards and..." And then he began biting his nails again.

I rolled over and closed my eyes. "Dad's been threatening to get away from it all for a long time," I said after a while.

"But we never believed him," argued Thomas. "He's been saying it for years."

"Maybe it's a mid-life crisis," I suggested,

opening my eyes a crack to see if this impressed him. This was something I'd recently heard about on the radio.

"What on earth's *that*?" said Thomas, looking at me scornfully. "You say some stupid things sometimes!"

"It's not stupid! I heard it on a talk-back radio programme," I said crossly. "Lots of grown-ups go a bit crazy when they think they're getting old. Makes them do weird things."

"Yeah? You mean other parents do this – this 'getting away from it all' thing?"

I thought back to the radio programme, with the jumble of voices all talking angrily. "I didn't listen for long. But that's what it's called – a mid-life crisis."

"But Mum and Dad have been talking about getting away from it all for years. For as long as I can remember they've been telling us about how great it was when they lived in that rickety, leaking caravan with Grandma and Grandpa, and went around the countryside, working as hard-up clowns..."

"And putting on Punch and Judy shows on the beaches and handing the hat round, like beggars..."

"And cooking sausages on the beach afterwards..."

"Because that was all they could afford..."

"And how happy they were even though

they didn't have enough money to go to the cinema…"

"Huddling under the blankets to keep warm in the winter…"

"Those were the good old days!" we both said together, and stared at each other in horror.

Thomas began biting his nails again. "I don't want to go back to the good old days. I want to stay in today!"

I decided to forgive his nail-biting. It was a nail-biting situation. You see, both our parents, Yasmin and Dylan, had had a weird, hippy sort of childhood. Well – weird to us, but they kept saying it had been great. Huh! And when they grew up, what did they do? Just the opposite, of course. They went to university. Dad became a brilliant computer scientist. Mum became a marine biologist. Then they got married and went to live in suburbia, where Thomas and I were born.

We liked it. We had a lovely house with a swimming pool. Mum lectured at the university and Dad did amazing things with computers. But they said they never really felt quite at home. Yasmin and Dylan became too successful. They had too many credit cards – too many consumer goods – too much of the good life. They felt uncomfortable, maybe even guilty.

For years, every few months Dad had been

coming home and saying "Yassie – we've got to get away!"

Mum would look at him with solemn eyes and say, "Oh, if only we could."

Thomas and I had heard this for so long that we never took it seriously. It was like hearing people talking about winning the lottery. Now suddenly it wasn't just pie in the sky.

"I can't believe they'd drag us back to that," I said miserably.

"We won't go!" said Thomas furiously. "We'll make them send us to boarding-school. I'm not giving up my Playstation!"

"Oh, Tommo, that's the least of our troubles. Imagine no central heating – washing in freezing water..."

"Well, some boarding-schools are a bit like that anyway," said Thomas gloomily. He put a hand over his eyes and almost looked as if he were going to cry. "No more Mr Nice Guy!" he whispered fiercely, one eye looking through his fingers. "We won't go!"

I rolled my eyes up at the ceiling at the idea of Thomas being Mr Nice Guy. But I was with him one hundred per cent. We were going to give them trouble!

But Mum and Dad just laughed when we told them we couldn't live without TV and computer games and stuff.

"Wait until you see what it's like," Dad said. "I promise you, if you hate it you can go to the boarding-school of your choice."

"Where is it, Dad – what's the big secret?" We were really puzzled. They never normally kept secrets from us. In fact, every decision about our lives was always endlessly discussed to death in boring family conferences, making sure all our feelings were expressed and ana-lyzed before anything got done. Thomas and I could see it made them happy so we went along with it, but most of the time we wished they'd just get on with it. We missed a lot of good TV that way.

"Wait and see," was all Dad and Mum would say.

So it wasn't until we actually landed on the island and saw the lighthouse for the first time that we knew where we were going to live – or why. But the moment we set eyes on it, we knew we'd never, ever want to go back to suburbia.

"Well – what do you think, kids?" asked Dad. We were gobsmacked. We stood, open-mouthed, gazing at the sight.

"Fantastic!" Thomas's voice hit the high registers of excitement. "This is the most incredible place you've ever taken us to, Dad. Where did you find it? Why are we here? How long can we stay?"

Dad just smiled. "And it's not even as if you deserve it, Tommo," he said. But he still hadn't answered the questions.

"Wow! Pol – look at it! Our own island! It'll be like being on holiday all the time!" Thomas ran around in circles, looking in every direction. "Look at the beach – look at the sea – how about those cliffs! I bet there are caves underneath…" He began running towards them.

"Hey – Thomas! – wait until we're unpacked!" Dad's voice was a command.

Thomas came back reluctantly. "You and Polly have to pull your weight now. There's only the four of us. No room for slackers!" he said firmly, and for once Thomas didn't answer back.

I couldn't take my eyes off the lighthouse. I'd never seen anything so beautiful and safe, standing tall and calm on the edge of the cliff. I couldn't wait to explore it. I realized in a blinding flash that it was exactly the sort of place I'd always wanted to live in – if I'd ever known it existed.

We'd been dropped by helicopter onto a helipad near the lighthouse. Dad had said we were only to take clothes and personal possessions – everything else would be supplied. So we had just a couple of suitcases each, which wouldn't take long to lug up to the front door.

The one exception to this rule had been Betty. There was no way we could bear to leave her behind, so Tommo and I had taken turns to carry her, miaowing and grumbling, in her pet carrier. We stood impatiently with our suitcases around us, waving goodbye to the helicopter, and as soon as it was off the ground we ran up to the front door while Dad fumbled with the key.

It's hard to believe it now, but at that moment, two years ago, when we stood on the doorstep waiting for Dad to open the door, I suddenly felt a flash of fear. We really were alone now, just the four of us – and Betty.

CHAPTER FOUR

The moment Dad opened the front door, we rushed up the stairs into the cheery kitchen, which looked as if it was part of a cosy farmhouse, and my fears disappeared. In fact, it had a warm, welcoming feeling – someone had obviously been getting ready for our arrival. At one end of the kitchen a large, old-fashioned cooker was already on, warming up the whole room.

"Oh!" exclaimed Mum. "An Aga! I've always wanted an Aga."

"What's so good about an Aga?" I asked.

"It's always warm – it stays on, day and night. Betty will love it." Mum lifted Betty out of the carrier and, sure enough, she sniffed at the warm oven door, sat right down beside it and began purring.

We couldn't wait to explore further. Up the winding staircase, from floor to floor, we ran.

Each new floor seemed better than the one before. There was even a huge food store in the basement, like a small supermarket, filled with all our favourite foods!

"Wow! Cool! Wicked! Totally awesome!" That was Thomas, almost hysterical with excitement. "Dad – why didn't you tell us how amazing it would be? It's got everything! Can we live here for ever…?"

"Take your suitcases up to the fourth floor – that'll be your room," said Dad, smiling at his enthusiasm. "You don't have to unpack immediately – come down to the kitchen. Mum and I will tell you all about it."

When we were all sitting in the kitchen with the kettle boiling for tea and hot, fresh-baked fruit scones on each plate with little golden, glossy, melting pats of butter on each half and Betty purring contentedly on my knee, Dad began.

"Although this lighthouse does exactly what lighthouses have done for centuries, it is not just a lighthouse," he said, looking serious. "Originally it was built on this island in the middle of dangerous shipping lanes, to constantly flash a warning light across the ocean, reminding ships not to come any closer to the rocks and reefs. It had a lighthouse-keeper and its own combination of flashes, rather like Morse code. Now, with modern technology, this isn't necessary. Computers have taken over all the work once done by humans—"

"I thought no one lived in lighthouses any more," Thomas interrupted, not properly listening and bored by all this talk. I could tell he desperately wanted to explore. "I remember our teacher telling us that."

"Be quiet and listen, Tommo. That's exactly what I'm trying to tell you," said Dad. "This is one of the last lighthouses to be operated by humans. But we're not simply lighthouse-keepers. That's why we were sworn to secrecy and couldn't tell you anything about it until now."

He paused and looked at us solemnly. "We've been sent here by a very important international organization to engage in undercover surveillance."

We sat up at that point. What had he said – had we heard right?

"Su – su – sur – veill...?" I stammered.

"You mean you're *spies*?" gasped Thomas.

"We're *all* spies," said Dad, and by the look on his face, we knew he wasn't kidding. "You and Polly and Mum and I. Our job is to help monitor the illegal trade in endangered animals and plants, and to be involved in intelligence-sharing with other operatives."

"Intelligence-sharing ... operatives ... what does it all mean?" I asked.

"A lot of what we will be doing will be processing and analyzing computer information sent to us. The information will help us to work out which animals and plants are most endangered, where they are being stolen from and who is stealing them. We will then pass this information on to other people in the organization who will be working with police and customs officials ... it's complicated. You don't need to know everything at the moment – but you will. Because you'll be part of it."

"You can't be serious!" gasped Thomas, still trying to take it all in. "Totally awesome!"

I didn't know what to say. I stared at my parents, calmly sipping tea and looking so ... *parentish*. Dad was a brilliant computer scientist – but a spy? And OK, Mum was a lecturer, but she'd always been so exactly like a typical Mum. She was brave (even though she was afraid of heights and scared of spiders) but I just couldn't see her as a spy.

Thomas stammered out the question in both our minds. "But – but – *why*? Why us? Why you and Mum?"

Mum laughed. "Don't you see me as a typical spy, Tommo?" she teased.

"No, I don't! You're – you're a mother..." His voice tailed off and he looked baffled.

"There are spies – and spies!" grinned Dad. "We're not exactly going to be involved in wartime espionage, like in the films ... although," his voice became serious again, "it is a war and there is an enemy. You see, the war is against the destruction of life on our planet – the life of animals and plants and us. And the enemy is anyone who kills endangered animals or poisons the water or cuts down the forests or pollutes the air."

"We're not alone in this fight," said Mum. "Over one hundred and fifty nations have signed a treaty to make the killing and trade in endangered animals and the cutting down of native forests and rare plants illegal. But laws don't stop criminals. If we don't do something, the endangered plants and animals will completely disappear. That's why we believe the organization is important."

"What's the organization called?" whispered Thomas, his eyes wide open with amazement.

"You don't need to know the name. In fact, it's better that you don't," said Dad sternly. "All I will tell you is that it is a large, international organization with a huge network of investigators, researchers and spies. Some of us help customs officials to identify parts of illegal animals and plants that people try to sell – tiger bone, rhino horn, bear gall bladders, orchids…"

"Why would people want to buy tiger bone or bear gall bladders?" I asked, with a shudder.

"There are some funny ideas in the world," said Mum. "In some countries, wild animals have been killed for hundreds of years just to get tiny parts of their bodies, which are believed to have healing powers."

"Some others – like us," said Dad, "are trained to help police in 'sting' operations, to catch smugglers. Other people in the organization actually infiltrate the underworld of wildlife smugglers…"

"Wow," Thomas gasped, "I'd like to do that!"

"Wait a few years, Tommo," grinned Dad. "It's pretty dangerous! There are huge forces out there being threatened by this war – evil dictators and wicked people with vast fortunes at stake—"

"That's why we couldn't say anything to you until now," broke in Mum. "No one must know the real purpose of our living here. We've got to look as if we're just a family opting out of ordinary life, fed up with the rat-race. We have to say we've decided to bring you children up on the island, away from the polluting influences of the cities. And, in a way, it's true. It will be a very different life here, from the one we've left." She looked at us anxiously. "I hope you won't be bored and lonely – that's the only thing that worries me."

"Lonely!" Thomas blurted out. "As if that would matter anyway. This is such a … a … an important thing to do. Saving the planet, I mean!"

"We couldn't possibly be bored," I said.

"There'll be so much to do – swimming, exploring…"

"Well, we'll see," said Mum thoughtfully. "We're contracted for two years. We'll see how you feel after that – more tea, anyone?" She poured herself another cup.

Dad passed his cup over and said, "As to why we were selected – well, think about it. Your Mum's a marine biologist and I'm a computer scientist. We had most of the necessary skills. All we needed was a course in sailing and navigation, which was why we went away on holiday without you last year."

I shuddered as I remembered the winter holiday with the grandparents in a chilly caravan. I went over to the window and sat on the wide ledge with Betty in my arms. We both looked out at the vast, silvery ocean. She miaowed gently and then reached up and patted my face as if to ask what we were looking for. The ocean looked completely empty.

"How will we do it?" I asked, gazing down at the emptiness. "Where will we get the information from? It won't be like neighbourhood watch – people won't just pop in and deliver notes to tell us who's up to dodgy tricks in the area."

"You can see a lot of things from a lighthouse," said Dad, "And if the lighthouse is packed with the latest in communication technology, you can discover a lot of things. You saw the communications room?"

We nodded, looking at each other with excitement. We were longing to learn how to use it all.

"That's the heart of the lighthouse, the room where all the information picked up via the Internet, e-mail, radar, satellite and any other means will be analyzed by the computers – and us – and will be transmitted to the organization."

"Cool!" said Thomas.

"We'll also be watching and reporting on passing shipping, monitoring ocean pollution and signs of illness in marine animals and plants, looking out for anything that could be dangerous or illegal..." began Dad.

"And there'll be lots of paperwork – too boring for you children – but absolutely essential to the battle," Mum continued.

"We're here to collect all the information we can, in order to help save the planet," Dad went on. "We have to keep our eyes and ears open for anything that could endanger life on earth. And you children have to help. You're part of the team."

"That's great by us!" said Thomas fervently, "Isn't it, Pol?"

"Oh, yes!" I could hardly believe we were going to be doing such exciting, important work. "Are you going to teach us to use the computers and the radar?"

"That'll be part of it," said Dad, "And you'll be helping with many other things too. But what you must remember at all times is that absolute secrecy is essential. We don't expect to see many people. There will be no one but ourselves on the island. Even the helicopter pilots delivering stores every three months don't really know what we're doing here. But if you ever come across anyone—"

"Who would we come across?" interrupted Thomas.

"Well, maybe shipwrecked sailors, or a yacht looking for a safe harbour for a few nights. There's a lot more going on out there than you'd think."

I looked out at the emptiness again and felt a slight chill creep over me. It looked so harmless at the moment. I hugged Betty closer.

"You'll both remember, won't you: secrecy at all times." We nodded. "If anyone asks you what your parents do, I'm afraid you'll have to tell a white lie. From now on, all you know about us is that we're both writers."

"I write about marine biology and your father is a technical writer and computer programmer," Mum broke in, "which is the truth of course – but not the whole truth. That way, you won't have to answer questions about what books we've written. OK?"

"Yes," we both said together.

"Now – the first thing you'll need to do is

familiarize yourselves with the island," said Dad, going over to the dresser and opening a drawer. "So before you go exploring tomorrow, take a good look at these maps – one for each of you." He gave us each a small, pocket-sized map and we spread them out on the table and began to pour over them. "Mind you take them with you tomorrow." We could hardly wait for morning.

I opened my eyes at sunrise, and immediately the memory of where we were and what was out there waiting for us exploded in my mind.

"Tommo! Wake up – let's explore!" I called, pulling on my clothes. We raced downstairs, gulped down a bowl of cereal, grabbed the packets of sandwiches that Mum had left for us, and, shutting a very cross Betty safely in the kitchen, flew downstairs and out the door.

The maps had shown us that the island was about five kilometres in diameter. It was wild and beautiful, with a forest, a small lake and a river, and sandy coves and rocky shores with colonies of seals and sea birds. We specially loved the seals. That first day we could see them playing on the beach and swimming in the sea. A few weeks later the baby seals arrived – so adorable with their soft white fur and big, dark eyes. That year we spent ages watching the mothers and babies playing together – the mothers feeding the babies and stroking their backs, not unlike human mothers and babies. Once upon a time they would have been hunted for their beautiful white fur. Hunting baby seals is now illegal, thank goodness.

But the most wonderful thing on the island was the castle – our very own castle! Dad had pointed it out on the map, telling us it was so ancient it must have been built during the Crusades. That first day we just had a quick look round it, deciding to explore it properly the next day.

And just as well because it took us nearly all day. The castle is large and stands on a cliff overlooking the sea. The walls are so high that the view is every bit as good as from the lighthouse. We imagined the soldiers standing there, watching their enemies coming closer across the sea. The soldiers would be heating the cauldrons of boiling tar and oil to spray on the enemies as soon as they got beneath the castle walls. We imagined the hordes of enemies screaming and falling back down the castle walls and into the sea as the boiling mixture got underneath their armour, causing terrible burns. It is a stunning and terrifying place. We just couldn't believe we were lucky enough to have it all to ourselves! But the whole island and everything on it was more wonderful than we could have ever imagined.

The third day we had to begin our school work: special lessons on the Internet. From then on we spent the mornings in the computer room or the library. But in the afternoons, unless Mum and Dad needed help, we could do whatever we wanted: swimming, boating, fishing, playing in the castle, roaming the island.

Wherever we go Betty comes with us. And later, when Squawkette grew big enough, she always came too. Always – until now. With Squawkette gone, it just wouldn't be the same anymore.

Thinking about Squawkette made me want to cry again. I shut my eyes, squeezing them tight to stop any more tears coming out. There was a soft thump on the end of my bed as Betty jumped up and padded gently over me.

"Mowow," she said, and touched her cold nose to mine, collapsing on my chest in a warm, purring mound with her head on my shoulder.

I felt a huge sob welling up in me. I put my arms around Betty, hugging her close, and fell asleep.

CHAPTER FIVE

I was woken up by Betty snoring like a little pig, right in my ear. I pushed her soft body away and gradually realized it wasn't night yet. I hadn't had supper. I felt horribly shivery and cold and depressed. Then I remembered about Squawkette. My heart started beating fast and I began to feel all hot and feverish. I wondered if by any chance there had been any hopeful news. I sat up. The wall had been pulled back – Thomas's bed was empty.

"Aow! aow!" Betty pounced on me, wanting to play as I scrambled out of bed. I picked her up and gave her a cuddle, rocking her in my arms like a baby. Her bright yellow eyes looked up unblinkingly, as if she was thinking serious thoughts. I kissed her funny little face. She was a "Tortie" Burmese – a mixture of colours, cream with smudgy greyish-brown markings and ears.

She was so intelligent, she was more like a person than a cat. We often said she was our minder. She always knew what we were up to and stayed on guard to warn us of any danger. She talked to us constantly, in a peculiar deep, croaking range of different miaows and noises that we'd learnt to understand. Actually, we were convinced she tried to imitate human speech. It had dawned on me one day, when she had come into the room and said "Aow."

"Hey – she said, 'hullo', I'm sure she did. Did you hear that, Tommo?"

"Mmm." Thomas picked Betty up, cradling her in his arms and looked into her eyes. "Are you trying to talk like us?"

She looked back at him, her little head on one side, and said "Aaah."

Squawkette was sitting on his shoulder as usual. She was always a bit jealous when he cuddled Betty.

"Betty, Betty, Betty!" she taunted, bringing her face close to Betty's and opening her beak a little, as if to bite. Betty lifted her paw as if to slap Squawkette, but Squawky turned her head around and Betty's paw just stroked her feathers instead. "Betty, Betty, Betty!" she croaked again, bobbing up and down, imitating the way we called her.

"Tommo – why can't a cat imitate other sounds, just like a parrot?" I asked. "After all, cats have brilliant hearing, just like birds."

44

"Hmm. She hears us come into the room and say hullo, so she makes a similar sound when *she* comes into a room," said Thomas, thinking it through. "Hey – maybe you're right. She thinks we're her family, so she's trying to speak like us."

We asked Mum what she thought and instead of laughing at us, she said, "Who knows? It's possible. All successful animals adapt to their environment."

After that we were convinced Betty was trying to learn human-speak and we found we could understand almost everything she said.

She loved playing with us. She was brilliant at chasing and hide-and-seek, and ball games, and she loved going for walks. But she also bossed us continually, waking us up every morning, nagging and miaowing when it was time to go to bed. If we were watching television she'd jump onto our laps, stare up at us and then pat our faces as if giving us a little smack. If we were playing a board-game she'd sit right in the middle of the board and upset all the pieces. It didn't matter how much we shouted at her, she would never give up, and in the end we'd just pack up and go to bed.

But she couldn't boss Squawkette. No matter how cross she got, Squawkette was quicker and more wicked. Betty seemed to think Squawky was a bad influence over us and every now and then they'd have an awful screaming match – usually when Betty was trying to get us to go to bed. As soon as she began miaowing, Squawkette would start bobbing up and down on Thomas's shoulder, screeching and taunting her.

Betty would yell "Aa, aa, aa, aa!" at Squawky, as if saying, "Bad, bad, bad, bad!"

"Bossy Betty, bossy Betty, bossy Betty," Squawkette would screech, dive-bombing her and squawking with delight as Betty tried to leap up and grab her. Then we'd have to dive into the fray, grabbing one or the other before they got hurt. But these were only family squabbles. Now that she was gone, Betty would really miss Squawkette.

"Where is Squawkette – where is she, Betty?" I murmured, looking sadly into her eyes.

"Aow, prrraow," she said comfortingly, almost as if she was trying to tell me not to worry.

Suddenly there was a huge commotion – the thunder of running feet and the sound of shouting voices. Thomas burst into the room.

"There's a boat being driven aground – on the rocks at the end of the cove!" he shouted. "We think it's a guy who was calling for help a while ago. Dad and I are taking the inflatable to see if we can save him…" And he was gone.

"I'll come too!" I called, dropping Betty on the bed and running down after him.

46

But he called out, "Stand by on the shore – we may need you to secure ropes!"

Mum was in the kitchen when I flew down and dashed to the door.

"Polly, Polly, Polly, you're not going out like that! Waterproofs and gumboots—!" she yelled after me.

As I came running back she held out a yellow hooded waterproof jacket, leggings and yellow rubber boots.

"Mum! For goodness' sake – I'm in a hurry!" I shoved my feet crossly into the leggings and boots and grabbed the jacket.

"Put your jacket on properly!" Mum bellowed. "You're not leaving this room until you do – and what's more, I'm coming with you!"

Only then did I notice that she was all ready in her waterproof gear with a pack on her back. Betty suddenly appeared and ran to the door, obviously imagining this was a family outing. Mum scooped her up and opened the door.

"Quick – run," she said, and followed me out, still holding Betty. At the last moment she turned and gently threw her back into the kitchen, slamming the door. We could hear Betty's furious yowl as we ran down the stairs.

CHAPTER SIX

Outside the wind and waves were still raging. The blast from the sea was so strong that we could almost lean against it. We had to fight to force ourselves forward, sea spray whipping our faces with icy arrows. We linked arms and slowly made our way along the cliff above the cove until we got to the narrow rope-lined steps set into the cliff side at the far end. Below us the waves were flinging grasping fingers against the cliff-face, as if trying to snatch us. Mum gave me a frightened look.

"Do you think you can climb down?" she yelled, cupping her hands to stop the wind carrying her voice away.

"Yes!" I wasn't too frightened – I felt I'd be all right as long as I clung to the rope. I waited for Mum to start climbing, but she just stood there, staring down, gripping the top of the rope railing, and it took a few moments for me to realize that she was actually frozen with fear.

"Mum – are you all right?" I asked.

She turned to face me – she was white. "Polly – I don't know if I can do it. It's so far down— Oh!" She was visibly shaking. She looked down the cliff again, into the wild waves. Her face seemed completely drained of colour. "I must do it – I must … Dad and Tommo need us," she murmured. She closed her eyes and began to take a step, trembling and clinging to the rope.

I was stunned. Then I remembered – her fear of heights. She never talked about it much, but she couldn't even bring herself to look out of the windows on the high floors of the lighthouse and she never went onto the viewing platform. No wonder she was so terrified now. I pulled her back.

"Wait a minute…"

I could see the orange and black inflatable lifeboat bobbing from wave to wave, down below. It hardly seemed to be making any headway at all, looking more like a helpless child's toy, completely at the mercy of the seas. At the end of the cove, a small yacht was being bashed, again and again, against the rocks. It wouldn't be long before it was smashed to matchwood. Every now and then I could see something bob up from inside the yacht. I realized it was a man, obviously trying to work out whether he should fling himself from the yacht and try to swim to the beach. But the beach had disappeared! There was nothing but seething waves, endlessly roaring and crashing against the side of the cliff. It looked hopeless. Even if the inflatable did get close enough to the yacht to rescue the man, would they make it back to safety through the violent seas to the mooring underneath the lighthouse? I knew it had already been a death-defying trip through the storm for Dad and Thomas, just to get where the yacht was. The seas seemed to be getting rougher by the minute. They'd never make it all the way back to the lighthouse.

Suddenly, I had an idea. "Mum – I've got to go down with a rope. It's the only hope."

"No – no! That's far too dangerous!" She wrenched one hand away from the rope railing and held me. "You'd be swept away into the sea – you can't go!"

"Mum – Mum – listen!" I pulled her back from the edge of the cliff behind the shelter of a tall rock and dragged her to the ground. "Only one of us can go. There's only room for one, on the steps. It's got to be me. You must stay here and be my anchor. I'll be all right with your help!" I began opening the pack on her back. I took out a large loop of mountaineering rope with clips at either end. "Look – here's what we'll do…"

I clipped one end onto the fastening at the back of my jacket and wound it round me, tying it securely. "Clip the other end to your jacket." She fumbled but her hands were too cold. I managed to get it securely onto her jacket, then wriggling on my stomach I unwound enough of the rope at Mum's end to loop it round the rock. "Stay behind here – don't move. Hold the rope fast!" I took another loop of rope from the pack and clipped the end of it to my jacket. "I'm going down the steps with this – Mum – are you listening to me?" she was almost speechless with fear, but she nodded her head. "You must stay here! I can't be swept away if you stay here and anchor the rope. It'll be all right!" I put my arms around her. "Daddy and Tommo depend on us!" I pressed my mouth to her cold, wet face.

Mum hugged me hard. Then she let me go and wrapped her arms around the rock.

I slithered over the top of the cliff and began the descent. I went down backwards, trying to look only at each step below and not at the sea. I had looped the spare rope over my back like a climber, and I clung desperately to the rope railing while the rope attached to Mum slowly unwound.

The wind shrieked, tugging and buffeting me so much that I didn't really have time to be frightened – it took so much energy just holding on. When I thought I was about halfway down, I turned to see how close the sea was.

I could see that the inflatable was now quite close to the yacht. Could they see me? Would they understand my plan? I waved furiously. There was no answering wave. I waved and waved again. At last an arm waved from the inflatable. It looked like Thomas. He'd work out why I was there – I was sure he would.

I could only go down a few steps further without being dangerously close to the sea, so I turned back to face the cliff and slowly, my foot groping for each step, went down as far as I could. Then I turned to face the ocean again. Carefully I clipped one end of the spare rope to the rope railing and slowly inched the coil off my back over my head, sticking my arm through the loop. Now it was just a matter of waiting.

A huge wave washed over me, slamming me back against the cliff and then almost sucking me over the edge. I clung on desperately, spluttering and spitting out the icy salt water. When I could see again, I saw that the inflatable had managed to get very close to the yacht. As I watched, the man on the yacht threw a rope over to it – but it fell into the sea nearby. I saw him haul it in, loop it up and wait his chance again.

Up and down the inflatable bobbed, sometimes closer, sometimes further away. At last a large wave took it close to the yacht. The man threw the rope with all his might, and this time it fell into the inflatable. I saw Dad grab it and attach the end to the inflatable. Then we all waited for the moment when the man would jump. The yacht crashed and smashed against the rocks, planks of wood now splintering off, leaping in the air as if the boat was flinging up its arms in desperation. The man crouched on the side of the yacht and finally, when I was almost screaming with frustration, he jumped and landed close enough, with the help of Thomas and Dad, to slowly haul himself into the inflatable as the waves surged and sucked at him.

My arms were aching with exhaustion. I could hardly bear to think about how I was going to get back up the cliff, but I shoved the thought to the back of my mind. I had to concentrate on now – fix my eyes on the inflatable, to check they understood my plan, and be ready to throw the rope.

The inflatable was slowly moving away from the yacht. Sometimes it was almost lost behind large waves – sometimes it bobbed up again, riding the crest of a breaker. I waved and waved, straining my eyes to see an answering arm, and finally I saw Dad waving to me. The inflatable came closer and closer. I was terrified. Would I be able to throw them the rope? Back on the mainland we'd had an old game of quoits which had belonged to Dad's grandfather. Now, watching the inflatable below, I tried to think of it as a quoit target. If only it would keep still!

At last it was close to the bottom of the steps. Dad stood up in the inflatable and yelled, "Polly – Polly – *throw!*"

I could hardly hear what he said. In fact, if it hadn't already been my plan, I probably wouldn't have understood him, but I stood up, grasping the rope railing in one hand, and held out the loop of spare rope. I watched and watched, to judge when the inflatable would bob closest – and threw!

"Please – please..." I prayed, closing my eyes as it fell. "...let them catch the rope!" I knew there was no way I had enough strength left to haul the rope in again and coil it up to re-throw. I opened my eyes and – miracle of miracles – Dad was clipping my rope to the inflatable! Now they had to get as close as possible to the steps and pull themselves up out of the water, to safety. I had no more rope. Even if I had, I couldn't have pulled them up. All they could do was secure the inflatable, so that if they fell back into the sea they could cling to it and try again. I would have to cling like a limpet to the rope railing, waiting in case I was needed to give someone a hand. It would be a totally feeble, exhausted hand, but perhaps it might just be enough.

The first one to leave was Thomas. He leapt into the water as the inflatable bobbed close to the steps and with the waves lifting him high, and flailing his arms madly, managed to get close enough to grab the rope railing. I tried to help him but soon realized I was only in the way. I turned and climbed back a few steps and he staggered up, trailing a rope from his jacket, waves lashing at every step.

"Good on you, Pol!" he gasped as he got close, "Where's Mum?"

"She's up on the cliff, anchoring me around a rock!" I couldn't tell him how frightened Mum was.

"Get back to her – get back to safety – best thing now," Thomas gasped.

I turned and began the dreaded ascent. I was so tired and so cold; my hands were white and numb, my eyes blinded with wind. My only thought was, "Keep going – keep going – keep going!" as I stumbled up the slippery steps, clinging to the railing on one side and Mum's rope on the other.

It flashed briefly through my mind how dreadful it would be if the railing gave way, and I was furious with myself for thinking of it. "Shut up – keep going – keep going!" I forced myself to say over and over, trying to block out every other thought. Close to the top my foot slipped and shot over the edge of the steps. I seized the rope even tighter – my hands now so numb, I could hardly feel it – and pulled myself back onto the steps again. It was torture – a nightmare of fear and cold and pain and roaring noise. Now I couldn't think about Thomas and Dad, I could only cope with my own terror. My breath came in painful gasps. My legs were like jelly. I could hardly force them onwards.

"Just a few more steps ... a few more steps ...a few more steps." I blocked out everything but that, and at last saw the grassy top of the cliff! I stumbled and scrabbled up the last steps and then, letting go of the railing, pulled myself up onto the clifftop.

Just as I got to the top, a blast of wind hit me from the front, knocking me backwards. I rolled over, slithered a few feet, the rope slipping through my numb hands and, dangerously close to the edge, grabbed at a scrubby tree with one hand and broke my fall. My knees were over the edge. The feeling of nothing but space was terrifying. I put my head down on the wet grass, and holding the tree with one hand and the rope with the other, burst into loud gasps of terror. I was, in fact, safe: I was still attached to Mum. But it didn't feel safe...

"Polly – Polly – Polly!" I could hear Mum shrieking from the rock. She couldn't move. I hadn't left enough rope for her to leave the rock. She had to stay as an anchor, watching me dangling on the edge of the cliff.

"It's all right darling – you'll be all right –

just be calm – move slowly – you'll be all right…" Mum's voice was hoarse with fear.

After a while I lifted my head. "Mum…" I whimpered, but the wind whipped the words from my mouth. She was so close. I realized that if I didn't try to make a move right now, my hands would be so numb that I would fall backwards. Slowly, painfully, I strained the last ounce of strength I had and pulled myself forwards, inching up enough to get my knees back on the clifftop. Then I wriggled and squirmed forward on my stomach until I was opposite the rock, and still too terrified to let the rope go, I called out to Mum, and fainted.

CHAPTER SEVEN

The next thing I knew was silence. No howling wind, no lashing rain – just a peaceful, cosy feeling as if I were floating on a centrally heated cloud. I opened my eyes and a circle of faces stared anxiously down. I was lying on the window-seat in the kitchen, still in my waterproofs.

"Oh good," I said faintly, "you're all safe." Betty jumped up and walked over my chest, purring and licking my face, and suddenly the room came alive with people's voices.

"Polly, Polly. You're the bravest girl ever!" That was Mum's trembly voice.

"Well done, Pol – well done!" That was Dad's voice, sounding as if he was making an important announcement.

"Gee, Polly – totally awesome – what a hero!" That was Tommo, who, for once, was looking at me as if he meant it.

"Heroine," I corrected, but nobody heard me in the din.

"What a star!" said another, unknown, voice in a deep, American drawl. "We couldn't have made it without you!" It was the sailor. He was very tall and looked nice: a bit scruffy and unshaven, but with crinkly eyes and a nice smile. He stretched out his hand. "Jeremy Wright," he said. "May I have the honour of making your acquaintance?"

I sat up and held out my hand. "Polly Pickford. How do you do." And then, "Gosh – I'm starving!" as ravenous hunger swept over me. I started to get off the window-seat but suddenly felt terribly faint again and had to lie back down.

Mum said, "What am I thinking of!" and went to the fridge. "We must all be starving – let's eat!" She began taking out cheeses and pâtés and plates of ham and putting them on the table. A large loaf of crusty white bread, just baked that morning, also appeared. "Take your coats off, all of you," she said.

Everyone began introducing themselves to the sailor and talking about the storm and how lucky we were to have escaped. He pulled off his life-jacket and was about to take off his big oilskin jacket underneath, when he suddenly clapped his hand against his chest and exclaimed, "Well – I'll be darned!" He looked at Mum. "Entirely slipped my mind.

I've brought a friend. I hope he won't be an imposition, Mrs Pickford. He's a bit under the weather, I'm afraid."

He reached into his jacket and pulled out a battered, bedraggled bundle of feathers and laid it on the table. A wrinkled eyelid slid up – a bright, suspicious eye looked round the room and suddenly the bundle gave a jerk and a little squawk. Thomas gave a screech and lurched forward, arms around the bundle as if trying to cuddle it without touching it.

"It's Squawkette – Squawkette!" I screamed, jumping up and flinging my arms around the surprised sailor.

Suddenly Mum was flinging her arms around him too – he seemed to disappear into a scrum of women and when he came up for air, looking even more rumpled and wind-blown, he gasped, "You know this guy?"

The room seemed to explode with laughter. Mum and I danced around the room in each other's arms, chanting "Squawkette! Squawkette!" Betty danced with us, miaowing and squawking herself, and Dad kept slapping Jeremy on the back, shouting, "Amazing! Incredible!"

Thomas just knelt by the table, his face as close to Squawkette as possible, crooning her name and stroking her. After a while he stood up and said, "You'll never know how much this means…" He swallowed a huge lump in his throat and began again. "It's just so fantastic … it's just incredible … I can never thank you enough…" He held out his hand and shook Jeremy's so hard and so long that the sailor had to wrench it away.

"That's OK, buddy. Hey – glad to help out," Jeremy murmured, still puzzled as to what had actually happened.

Dad picked up Squawkette and held her against his shoulder, murmuring words into the little face. "He certainly won't be an imposition, Jeremy. He's a she, by the way, and we thought we'd never see her again." He held out the parrot's foot to Jeremy. "Squawkette's the name, and I know she'd shake hands with you if she could, but I don't think she feels much like being sociable at the moment."

Squawkette's eyes flashed up at Dad and then down at Betty, now standing on her hind legs, sniffing up at her. "Bossy Betty – bossy Betty," she croaked feebly and then closed her eyes.

Amidst the laughter, Mum appeared with a bottle of champagne. Dad opened it and Mum poured us all a glass – well, just half a glass for Tommo and me. We drank a toast to Jeremy, and then the questions just tumbled out: How – when – *where* did you find Squawkette?

"Hold on," he said, when he'd had a sip of champagne. "First I want to know how, when and where did you *lose* her?"

We filled him in on those dreadful details in a few seconds. And then he began:

"Well, it's an ill wind that doesn't blow somebody some good. If I hadn't been been asleep while the storm was approaching, I'd have taken my sails in sooner. But by the time I woke up, I had to really work fast to get them down in time. I was just pulling in the last sheet – it was flapping like crazy – when I felt this thump on the canvas and something fell down, right at my feet. I thought maybe it was a gull. I didn't look to see what it was until I'd gotten that last sail in. Then I picked it up, stuffed it in my jacket and went below. After I'd battened down the hatches, I pulled it out – and hey – that bundle of feathers was a parrot! I laid it on the table and thought, well, buddy, you've flown your last flight! I felt real sorry for it. It's feathers were battered and it looked like one of the wings and the tail feathers were broken. I got a towel and wrapped it round the body, to dry the feathers a little. Then I unwrapped it and tried to gently flex the broken wing. I lifted one of the eyelids and – hey – the pupil suddenly dilated and then focused on me. I'll be darned – it was alive! Then the other eye opened, and that bird gave a kinda shudder and a croaky squawk, and I thought, well, whadda you know – I think you'll pull through, buddy. You're one tough parrot!"

"Oh, Squawkette – Squawkette – you're so brilliant!" Thomas couldn't help but interrupt at that point.

"Sure is," said Jeremy, laughing. "But its troubles weren't over yet. The boat was starting to behave like a bucking bronco, so I put him – I mean, her – on the table in my cap, to make her safer if the boat rolled. Then I thought I'd better try to find something for her to eat, but I didn't know what. Maybe she lived on fruit and nectar, or maybe she's a meat-eating parrot – insects and stuff – I had no idea. So I got down a jar of honey and a can of corned beef and mixed them together. Then I thought what if she only eats seeds? Oh, what the heck – she's probably past saving, anyhow. But I added a dollop of peanut butter, stirred it all up and held it close to her face. First off, she just lay there, eyes closed – not a flicker. Then one eye opened, looked up at me, and – whadda you know? She pulled herself up and dipped her beak into the mixture. She perched there, looking sort of shell-shocked, keeping a beady eye on me. Then she opened her beak and that little tongue darted into the food, and I'll be darned if she didn't lift up her foot and scrape at some of the mixture ... made me laugh, I can tell you. And then suddenly I wasn't laughing anymore. There was a terrible lurch and a crashing noise, and I knew we'd run aground. That was when I made that mayday call ... and I reckon you know the rest."

We had the greatest celebration that day. We drank toast after toast to each other. We told each other over and over again exactly what we felt like as we battled with the storm – how at times we all thought we'd never make it. It was so great to be alive, to be warm, to be eating wonderful food – and most of all, to have Squawkette back again.

Mum examined Squawkette's poor wing; it was certainly broken. She moved it gently back and forwards while Squawkette lay looking forlorn and making the occasional protesting squawk.

"There's only one thing for it, I'm afraid," Mum announced ruefully. "She'll have to be strapped up."

"Her wing, you mean?" asked Thomas, frowning.

"Yes, her wing and her whole body," said Mum. "Unfortunately you can't just put a bird's wing in a splint. I'll put the wing in a sling and then band it gently to the body. But first I have to make sure the broken bones are properly aligned. And the sooner the better. Hold onto her while I get the first-aid box."

Squawkette lay on her back on the table, looking pathetically funny with her feet in the air, while Thomas gently stroked her poor wrecked feathers. "She looks as if she's had an argument with an egg-beater," he said sadly.

"That's not far off it," said Jeremy. "Can't believe she has any feathers left at all!"

"Will she be able to fly properly again?" I wondered.

"We won't know for several weeks. Now – you'll have to hold her tightly, Tommo," said Mum, sitting down at the table with the first-aid box. "It's not going to be easy. She won't like it much."

Gently she straightened the broken bone and then folded the wing back into position while Thomas held Squawkette's body as firmly as possible without squeezing her too much. It was surprising how co-operative she was. It must have been painful, but she only squawked a couple of times and gave several feeble jerks. Then she sat quite still, her beak open and her eyes looking warily at Thomas and Mum.

Mum made a long slit in a piece of bandage and slipped this over the folded wing, tying the ends firmly around several times so that Squawkette wouldn't be able to move it. Then she strapped the wing against Squawkette's body with masking tape. She looked so funny that we couldn't help laughing. Finally Mum cut off the broken tail feathers, leaving just stumps, like scruffy paint brushes, sticking out.

This was the last straw. Poor Squawkette!

Her dignity was really hurt. She gave a loud, angry screech, her eyes glaring furiously at us while we laughed and laughed.

"What about her tail feathers – will they grow again?" I asked.

"The broken bits will fall out when she moults and new feathers will grow after about six weeks," said Mum putting her gently in the cage. "She'll have to stay there for quite some time, I'm afraid."

Slowly, painfully, clinging with her beak and her feet, Squawkette climbed the bars of the cage until she got to the highest perch.

"Squawk," she croaked, looking at us all with her head on one side. Her eyelids began to close and she gave another small, moaning squawk, trying to tuck her head under her wing. One eyelid flew up crossly and she peered closely at the bandage. Then, as if she was just too tired to care, she hooked her beak into the bandage and went to sleep.

"Ohhhh," said Mum, yawning, "I know just how she feels."

I noticed suddenly that I was swaying back and forwards slightly, I was so tired. I shook my head and looked around the room. Thomas was almost asleep on the table, and Dad and Jeremy were dozing off too.

"Off to bed, everyone," said Mum standing up. "Tommo – make sure there's plenty of food and water in the cage."

66

As Thomas filled Squawkette's dishes I heard Mum telling Jeremy he'd have to sleep on a sofa in the sitting-room, and I was aware of Dad slipping quietly upstairs – no doubt to lock the communications room.

"It's going to be tricky," I whispered to Thomas as we stumbled upstairs. Mum was making up a bed on the sofa and explaining to Jeremy that we didn't have a spare bedroom – she hoped he'd be comfortable – and that tomorrow Dad would contact the rescue helicopter and he'd be airlifted back to the mainland.

"Of course. We've got to make sure he doesn't find out our secret! How are we going to work it?" whispered Thomas, as it dawned on him for the first time that the very situation we had thought least likely to happen – a stranger inside the lighthouse – was now a fact. "Wow, is it ever going to be tricky! I guess Dad'll work it out, though," he added as he fell into bed.

"Mmmm – Dad'll work it out," I murmured as my head hit the pillow. The last thing I heard was Betty's answering "Mprrrrrr, mprrrrr, mprrrrr."

CHAPTER EIGHT

When I woke up the next morning I was amazed to see how late it was. Thomas was still asleep. How come our usual alarm clock – Betty – hadn't woken us up? I scrambled into some clothes and ran downstairs.

Mum and Jeremy were sitting at the breakfast table. He had the slightly "wish-I-hadn't" look of someone who's eaten too much. He had his hand on his stomach and was saying, "No, really – I couldn't possibly..." but his voice faded as Mum ignored him and poured him another cup of coffee.

"Morning, darling," she said, smiling too brightly. "You've had a nice long sleep."

"Hi – how's Squawkette?" I went over to the cage and looked at her. What a mess. Her beak was still tucked into the bandage and she seemed to be asleep, but she opened one eye and looked at me glumly and then made a disgusted sort of "bluh, bluh" noise, as if she was about to be sick.

"She's all right," said Mum. "Still in shock, I shouldn't wonder."

"Great breakfast. Wonderful coffee," Jeremy was murmuring. "You lighthouse-keepers have it good."

Mum smiled and passed him the cream and sugar. "More toast?" she asked.

He shook his head firmly, protesting again that he couldn't possibly, and I noticed in a quick glance how clever she had been. Usually we had magnificent breakfasts – sometimes truly inventive: pizzas and hot dogs and pan-cakes with maple syrup and crispy American bacon and chocolate croissants, all in one glorious feast. With our super-tech storeroom, we could have anything we wanted. But this morning there was just toast and marmalade on the table – nothing that would cause undue speculation.

"I'm starving! Tommo's still asleep," I said, and helped myself to toast.

"Make yourself some fresh, dear," Mum said vaguely. "Yes – I made sure you could both sleep late this morning." She cast a wry glance at Betty, sitting on a cushion in front of the Aga.

"Yassie!" I teased in Dad's voice, "you'll spoil that cat!"

"Anything to keep her down here rather

than waking you up. You must be so tired after yesterday."

"Yes – how is our star this morning?" asked Jeremy. "Must have a few aches and pains. I'm sure you don't rescue stranded sailors from the teeth of a storm every day of the week!" He smiled quizzically, and I wondered if there was a hidden meaning behind the innocent-sounding question.

"N … no – not often," I began cautiously.

"I suppose you're wondering what we're doing here and why we're so well equipped?" said Mum with a nervous smile as she helped herself to another piece of toast.

"Well, I must confess I was rather surprised to discover a manned lighthouse in this day and age – complete with lifeboats and brave lighthouse-keepers, too. Not that I'm complaining," he added, shaking his head seriously. "Wouldn't be alive to complain if it hadn't been for your courage and kindness – all of you."

"I'm a marine biologist, working on a book about marine ecosystems," said Mum between popping snatches of hastily buttered, marmaladed toast into her mouth. "And Dylan is a technical writer and computer programmer. When we were offered this lighthouse for a few years, it seemed ideal." I noticed her hand was shaking slightly. "We wanted to get away from the problems of city life. Lovely place to bring up the children..." She was blushing slightly; I knew how difficult she found it to tell even the whitest, white lie.

"It's an absolutely wonderful place to live!" I broke in hurriedly – anything to divert attention from the lighthouse itself. "The island, I mean. We've got everything. A lake, a forest, fantastic beaches, amazing wildlife – even a castle..."

"Perhaps you'd like to show Jeremy around, with Thomas, after he's had his breakfast?" Dad said, coming quietly into the room. I realized he must have been listening outside the door. "Take him down to see the seal colony. The babies have just been born. They're so cute at the moment with their white fur. Quite an experience," he said, turning to Jeremy, "to see the mothers feeding and cuddling their calves."

"I'd like to see that," said Jeremy.

"But in the meantime we should go out to the yacht as soon as possible, to collect what we can of your things."

"Sure – if there's anything worth collecting," said Jeremy.

"The sea's like glass out there today," said Mum, looking out the window. "It's hard to believe it was so dreadful yesterday."

"As soon as you've finished breakfast, I'll take you out in the inflatable," said Dad, obviously keen to get Jeremy out of the house as quickly as possible.

"And when you come back you can do a tour of the island with Polly and Thomas," said Mum, beginning to clear the table in a rather obvious way. "By that time the rescue helicopter should have arrived!"

"Um – well – OK." Jeremy gulped down his last few mouthfuls of coffee. "That's it, buddy," he said, standing up. "We're outta here!" He gave a Dad a mock salute. "Thanks for that terrific breakfast, Yasmin." He followed Dad out the door.

"Mum – wait a bit – I haven't finished!" I wailed as she cleared away my plate while I was still eating.

"Oh, sorry." Mum brought it back and collapsed into a chair, her voice dropping to a whisper. "I'm just so worried. What if he finds out? It's so hard to … to…"

"Lie, you mean?" I grinned. "I always thought you'd make a rotten spy – you're just not up to it!"

"Oh dear!" Mum looked anxious for a moment and then gave me a swipe. "I'm not ashamed of being a bad liar. It's a pity more people don't have the same problem!"

"Just leave it to Tommo and me – we'll lie through our teeth if we have to, buddy!"

She laughed at my imitation of Jeremy. "He seems a nice chap. Very pleasant and easy-going. I must say I rather like him, but…" She was serious now. "I can't help wondering why he was sailing so close to the island. When you take him around, make sure you are very careful not to mention a word that would make him suspicious. His easy-going act may be bogus. He could be spying on us, for all we know!"

"Why? Who'd he be working for?"

"Oh – there are so many possibilities. You've heard of industrial spies?"

I nodded. "Dad was always talking about industrial espionage when he was working for those computer companies."

"There's so much money to be made from the destruction of the environment, and so many greedy people out there who won't stop at anything. They're prepared to lie and cheat and even kill, if anyone gets in their way." She looked grim. "I should remember that when I find it difficult to tell a few white lies!"

Thomas clattered down the stairs and into the room. "Mum – why did you let me sleep so late?" He was looking cross. "Where is everybody? Where's Betty? Why didn't you wake me up?" Betty looked up and miaowed sleepily. "You spoiled thing!" he said, glaring at her snuggling comfortably in front of the Aga. "How's Squawkette?" He ran over to the cage and pressed his face against the bars. Squawkette opened a tired eye and gave a weary croak. "You look like something the cat dragged in," he said gloomily.

Betty opened her eyes, looked at him reproachfully and yawned, turning away with disgust.

"Charming! A positive ray of sunshine, I must say!" Mum looked at him sarcastically over the top of her glasses.

He sat down at the table looking sullen. "I feel ... lousy," he said.

She leaned across and gave him a hug. "You're tired, that's all. It was such a terrible strain yesterday, it'll take you a while to get over it. Have some breakfast. I'll make you a big mug of milky coffee. Polly, make him some toast."

"He can make his own!" I said crossly.

"Only toast?" He looked aghast. "I'd like sausages and eggs and..."

"Use your head, Tommo – we don't want to make someone suspicious." I got up and put two thick slices of bread to grill on the Aga, looking at him meaningfully.

"Oh, yes." The implications of yesterday came flooding back.

"Here – I've put your toast on for you, you can watch it. Don't let it burn," I said, sitting down to my coffee again.

Thomas got up reluctantly and stood over the Aga. "Where is he – Jeremy, I mean?"

"Gone with Dad to his yacht, to collect his

74

things. When he comes back you and I are taking him for a tour around the island."

"I don't feel like it…"

"You will when you've had some breakfast," said Mum, putting a large, steaming mug on the table in front of him. "It's just shock, like poor old Squawkette. You'll feel better soon."

"Squawkette's lucky. She can just sit on her perch all day," grumbled Thomas as he stirred his drink. He took a couple of sips and began to look brighter. "Are you really suspicious of him, Mum?" he asked after a while.

"Well, Tommo – as I've just been telling Polly, we can't take any chances."

"But he did save Squawkette," Thomas pointed out.

"That doesn't prove anything," I said. "He didn't know Squawkette was ours. And he didn't save her on purpose. It was just … good luck."

"I guess…" Thomas looked thoughtful. "What was he doing near the island, anyway? Do you think he'd been sent to spy on us? Maybe he's working for the enemy?"

"It's possible," said Mum, looking worried. "So you must be extra careful not to give anything away. I'm sure he's not dangerous – I mean – he wouldn't do you an injury. There's no reason for him to do that. If he is spying for an enemy organization, that would only blow his cover. I wouldn't send you off with him if I thought he was dangerous. But he might try to get information from you. You must be very careful what you say."

"Yes, yes, Mum. Sure," Thomas said, irritably. He hated being nagged. After he'd munched his way through several huge slices of hot buttered toast and blackberry jelly, he became quite cheerful. "OK," he began to plan. "First we'll take him to the lake, then the forest, then the seal beach and finally the castle…"

"Why not walk around the beach first, then go back via the castle, the forest and the lake…?

"No – let's leave the castle till last, it's the best…"

"I think you should plan the longest route," Mum interrupted. "The whole idea of this tour of the island is to keep Jeremy away from the lighthouse for as long as possible. It would be ideal if he could arrive back to find the helicopter waiting. Then he could just be whisked away without any further ado."

"Do you know when the helicopter will arrive?" asked Thomas.

"Not exactly. They said late afternoon. I'd better pack a picnic." She stood up. "Come and help me get some food from the storeroom, Polly – quick – before Dad and Jeremy get back."

Mum closed the door of the storeroom on us after we went in, and locked it. "Just to guard against accidents," she said. "If he got a look at all this exotic food, he'd think it very strange for a simple family living an alternative lifestyle. Now what shall we choose... What would be unsuspicious?" She picked up a large canned ham and then a bag of frozen bread rolls. "I'll defrost them in the microwave – they look as if they're home-made, don't you think?" she asked.

I couldn't tell. "Does it really matter, Mum? Surely he wouldn't notice things like that."

"We don't know what he might notice. If he's a spy, he'll have been trained to notice all sorts of things."

"But wouldn't it be logical for us to have shop-bought bread rolls in the freezer?" I asked stubbornly.

"No," said Mum firmly. "Takes up too much room. In a place as isolated as this, freezer space would usually be kept for meat and milk. Bread would always be home-made..." Her voice trailed off as she walked around looking for inspiration. I was bored. Mum always got bogged down with these silly details. Finally she loaded me up with half a cheddar, some apples and half a dozen eggs.

"Pretty boring, if you ask me," I said, thinking of the packs of yummy prepared garlic breads and filled croissants, not to mention the savoury tarts, bacon and egg pies and all sorts of cold meats and quiches that we usually took on picnics.

"Come on – quickly! Be ready to run upstairs the moment I make sure the coast is clear." Mum opened the door a crack and peered out, listening for voices. "OK." She beckoned to me and I ran up while she locked the door and followed.

By the time Dad and Jeremy arrived back from the yacht with the few of his belongings that had still been salvageable, Mum had made a nice – but ordinary – picnic of cheese and ham rolls, hard-boiled eggs and apples.

"Wow. What a marvel! Such wonderful food at the drop of a hat!" said Jeremy as he took charge of a pack. Tommo and I grinned at each other. What would he say if he could see what he was missing!

CHAPTER NINE

As we walked along, I found myself beginning to agree with Mum that Jeremy was really rather nice. He had offered to carry our lunches in his backpack, which was one of the few things he had salvaged from the yacht, but Thomas had said "no thank you," just in case (he told me later) Jeremy was a spy and would run off with his food, leaving him starving and weak. I'd said "no thanks," because I didn't like the mouldy, salty smell of his backpack. Betty, as usual, had insisted on coming with us and either ran along in front hiding and waiting for us to arrive so she could jump out at us, or dawdled behind, stalking some fascinating leaf or insect. Every now and then she'd catch up and pass us, tearing along, leaping over tall grasses with her tail held high in a big round curve. She seemed to rather like Jeremy, too, because she often ran up and bounced off his legs and then dashed madly away, hoping he'd chase her. He did, once or twice, and I could see Thomas looking at him suspiciously. Jeremy had insisted on carrying the bag of crunchies that Mum had given us for Betty. Thomas was worried. He fell behind and yanked at my arm, signalling that he wanted a private word.

"You don't think he'll do something tricky with Betty's lunch, do you?" he whispered. "Use it to lure her to her death, or something?"

"Why?" It sounded a stupid idea to me.

"Maybe he's planning to put the frighteners on us!" Thomas hissed in a phoney accent, pretending to be a TV detective.

"You must be joking!" I said scornfully, thinking Jeremy couldn't look less like a heavy if he tried.

"A joke?" Jeremy's head swivelled round. "Come on – let me in on it. Nothing I like more than a good joke!"

"Um … er … why did the prune go out with the raisin?" I gabbled, gazing at him like a startled rabbit. I felt quite jumpy – he did have super-sharp ears!

"I don't know," he said, grinning.

"Because it couldn't get a date," I said faintly.

"Polly – that's feeble," snapped Thomas.

"Is it?" Even if it was feeble, would it matter if I told a feeble joke to a spy? "Well, what

80

about, "Where do fishes keep their money?" I began lamely.

"Oh, forget it," Thomas growled and I shrugged away, catching up with Jeremy, who was laughing. I could feel Thomas's furious gaze boring into my back. He was really working himself up now. He stayed a few steps behind us, no doubt so he could keep an eye on Jeremy. I knew what would be going on in his mind. "If Polly's gone over to the enemy," he'd be thinking, "it's all up to me. I'll have to stay super-alert." Honestly – sometimes Tommo was a pain!

The sun was hot as we walked along and I struggled to take off my coat, getting tangled up in the lining. Jeremy helped me and insisted on putting it in his backpack, saying, when I thanked him, "It's the least I can do after what you did for me yesterday, little Polly Pickford."

I didn't much like being called little, but I knew he was just trying to be kind. I sneaked a sideways glance at him. I really couldn't believe he was a spy. He seemed too ... laid back. But if Mum suspected him, I'd better be extra careful. He saw my look and smiled.

"Liked your joke, by the way," he said reassuringly. "Know any more, buddy?"

"I'm not very good at jokes," I said truthfully. "I usually get them wrong. Thomas is better than me." Then I said, "I'm quite good

81

at riddles, though." This wasn't true – I could never remember jokes or riddles. I don't know why I said it. Perhaps it was something to do with the fact that I was getting more and more nervous, what with Thomas being horrid and the thought that we were walking further and further away from safety with someone who might be an enemy.

"Go on then – ask me a riddle."

I thought hard and then remembered the first one I'd ever read for myself, in a comic, which had stayed in my mind because I had been so amazed, as I'd watched the sentence unfold, at being able to read it all the way to the end. "What's the difference between a mad Dutchman and a pipe?"

"Um..." He thought for a while. "I give up!" he said at last, pretending desperation.

"One's a silly Hollander and the other's a hollow cylinder."

He laughed again and I felt better.

"That's very clever," he said admiringly. "You're all very clever – a clever family. What are you going to be when you grow up – a marine biologist, like your mother?"

"No, I don't think so. It's quite interesting, marine biology, but I think I'd rather be a film star."

"Hmm." He thought about that for a while. "Hard work, being a film star, I should imagine." And then, as quick as a wink, he slipped in, "What sort of marine biology does your mother do?"

I felt a surge of fear. He was trying to trap me. "She writes – about dolphins and things. Like Flipper, you know?" I said vaguely, putting on a slightly dumb voice. And then before he could reply, I said, "Have you ever seen *Jaws* – isn't it scary? Mum knows all about sharks and things."

"Hmm," he said.

"And did you know that the Russians and the Americans have taught dolphins to find enemy mines and stuff – you know – in war situations? Only the Russians are better. They've taught their dolphins more tricks. And they give them state burials when they die."

"Well, I'll be darned! Sounds like you've swallowed an encylopedia," he said, laughing.

I didn't know whether he was being rude or nice. I began to say something else about dolphins, but then Betty hurtled past at breakneck speed and ran round in circles before shooting up a tree and calling to us from the branches.

"What an amazing cat!" he interrupted. "Can't imagine how you get her to perform such tricks! Maybe you should join a circus – be an animal trainer?"

"No thanks. I don't much like circuses," I said.

"Well, well! Neither do I," said Jeremy.

"You and I have a lot in common."

"I went to one once, and I thought the animals looked sad. And I hated the clowns!"

"Really?"

"I was frightened they'd throw water over me."

"You surprise me, Polly Pickford. I didn't think you'd be frightened of anything!" he said smiling down at me admiringly. I must say I began to feel rather – well – special. It was a nice change from Thomas's nag, nag, nag, always telling me I was doing everything wrong, or I was stupid, or I was a baby...

"Polly – watch where you're going!" Thomas's voice suddenly blasted out, bringing me down to earth with a thump. I looked around and realized I was going in the wrong direction, and taking Jeremy with me. His sweet-talking had made me careless.

The plan was to go anti-clockwise around the island, down through the forest to the lake, and then in a zigzag route to the castle, where we'd have lunch. Then we'd walk back around the eastern shore, along the beach and cliffs, to the lighthouse. We thought we'd probably be able to see the helicopter as we approached, and could slow up if there was still no sign of it.

We'd already walked through the forest and round the lake and were now supposed to be heading towards the castle when I'd begun to go the wrong way. I ran back to Thomas, getting close enough to whisper crossly, "Sorry – he's asking me questions and I'm doing my best to put him off the track – it's not easy!" I felt as if Thomas was letting me shoulder the burden of Jeremy all by myself. He might at least keep up with us and do some of the talking.

"Just watch yourself – that's all!" Thomas hissed. "Don't go shooting your mouth off."

"Oh, shut up. You're not helping at all."

"Well, where is he now?" Thomas suddenly demanded. Jeremy was nowhere to be seen. "Polly – can't you be trusted to get anything right?" He began frantically peering in every direction. "If we've lost him it'll be all your fault!"

"He was with me a moment ago," I wailed, looking distractedly around. I couldn't believe he'd disappeared so quickly. "It's not my fault. You weren't even trying to talk to him. You went off by yourself, sulking as usual!"

"Shhh! What was that?" Thomas grabbed my arm and slapped a hand across my mouth. In the silence that followed we heard a twig snap and then suddenly Jeremy emerged from the gloom of the bushes, looking rather pleased with himself.

Thomas let go of me, murmuring, "How long has he been hiding there, listening?" and stared menacingly at Jeremy.

But Jeremy looked blandly cheerful. "Lead

on, McDuff!" he said to Thomas. "I'm looking forward to seeing this castle of yours."

And then I noticed someone else was missing. "Has anyone seen Betty?" I asked, realizing we hadn't seen her for quite some time.

"This is just what I've been waiting for!" hissed Thomas in my ear, "It's obviously a plot of some sort to ... to..." But he couldn't think what it would accomplish. "It's deeply suspicious!" he whispered furiously.

"She's probably just..." I began, but he wasn't listening, he'd started hunting around frantically.

"Why weren't you taking better care of her?" he yelled at me.

"She's just as much your cat as mine – why weren't *you*?" I shouted.

We both glared at each other furiously and then began shouting, "Betty ... Betty ... Betty ... come on, come on..." calling loudly in all directions.

"I'll go back. You two stay here in case she's nearby," he barked, running back down the track.

"She's usually so good and sensible. She comes everywhere with us..." I began miserably, and was about to say, "She usually looks after us," but it occurred to me that maybe this information could put Betty in danger, so I quickly shut up. It was so hard having to think twice about everything I said.

Jeremy ambled towards the edge of the lake. "What's that – there?" he said, pointing at a ripple on the surface, coming slowly closer. "Good Lord!" He shadowed his eyes, peering hard. "I think it's Betty..." He began stripping off his trousers. "Sorry about this," he said. "Close your eyes if you're offended – I'm going in."

I was too shocked and worried about Betty to care whether I saw Jeremy's underpants. Now I could see little ears and a nose sticking out of the water, as, slowly and clumsily, Betty swam closer and closer to shore.

"Betty – Betty – come on – come on – come on!" I called loudly, "Don't give up – don't give up..." I held my breath with fear as every now and then the little head disappeared beneath the water. She was obviously getting very tired.

Jeremy was wading up to his waist now, and was almost within reach of her. Just a few more seconds and then he scooped her out of the water, dripping and crying. She slithered out of his grasp, drenching him with water and climbing as high up his body as she could, but he held her firmly against his shoulder until they got to shore. I held out my arms for her, but Jeremy put her on the ground.

"Better let her try to shake some of the water off," he said. "No point in you getting soaked too."

I was so grateful. "Oh, thank you, thank you!" I felt really sorry for thinking anything bad about him. Surely he couldn't be a spy, he was so kind! I was positive Mum must be wrong.

"Here." He threw me a scrap of towel he had been drying himself with. "Give her a rub-down with that." I picked it up gingerly – it smelt rather like the backpack it had just come out of – and grabbed Betty, who was franti-cally trying to lick herself dry, and rubbed her hard.

"You've found her!" Thomas appeared, breathing hard. "Where was she? She's soak-ing!" He picked her up and Betty immediately licked his face, miaowing excitedly, as if trying to tell what had happened.

"She was in the lake, swimming for dear life." Jeremy was doing up his belt. "Jeremy waded in and saved her. She was nearly drowned! Honestly, if we hadn't seen her I don't think she'd have made it. Jeremy saved her!" I said loudly.

"Glad to be of help," said Jeremy. "A mere nothing compared to what you two did for me yesterday."

"Thanks," said Thomas, looking suspi-ciously at Jeremy. "But how did she get in there?" He gave me an angry glance. "Got any ideas?"

"Nope," I shrugged. "Unless she climbed a

88

tree and fell in?"

"No idea." Jeremy shook his head, appearing genuinely mystified. "Seems unlikely she could have got so far out, just falling from a tree."

"Maybe she tried to catch a fish, which dragged her into the middle of the lake?" I said.

"Oh, don't be so stupid!" Thomas dismissed this instantly. "You do talk rot! I don't know..." he continued, looking worried. "Maybe we'd better just go home."

"She looks quite dry, now," I pointed out coldly, "and it's nearly as far to go back as to go on. I think we should go and have lunch at the castle. I'm starving." I picked up my bag of lunch and walked off. I was really fed up with Thomas.

He caught up with me. "Don't you see? It must be his fault!" he whispered furiously. "While our backs were turned he must have thrown Betty in."

"I don't believe it!" I said, looking at him stubbornly. "He was the first one to see her in the lake. He took off his trousers and waded in. If he'd thrown her in, he'd never have pointed her out. He'd have diverted my attention and taken me further away from the lake. Anyway, what's his motive? She's only a cat. Why would he want to kill her?"

Thomas was silent. He couldn't really think

up a valid reason, he was just suspicious. "Who can tell what evil lurks in the hearts of men," he said darkly. "Only the Shadow knows!" This was something Dad often said, a quotation from one of the radio serials he'd listened to when he was young.

"Well, you're not the Shadow, and don't think you are!" I said crossly. "And I think Jeremy's kind and nice and not a bit like a spy. So there!"

"He's really got you fooled, hasn't he," said Thomas bitterly. Betty was struggling to get down now, so he set her free. "Just don't forget to keep your eyes peeled. All the time."

CHAPTER TEN

The castle loomed up in front of us, standing tall and defiant, overlooking the sea on the highest point of the cliff. Usually it promised security – an ancient haven of safety against enemies. Today it seemed to me that it looked menacing and sinister. We were walking up the zigzag path to the top of the hill, the motte. Thomas was still trailing behind with Betty, who seemed quite tired after her swim, on his shoulder.

"Hey!" said Jeremy admiringly, mopping his head as he looked at the castle. "Must have been a great deal bigger at one time. Only the keep left now."

"Dad says it was probably only ever a fort," I said. "It's too remote here, to have had a lord and his family living in it – only soldiers.

An outer wall ran around the keep, now crumbling and broken in parts. We passed through the arch, which had long since lost its huge gates.

"This is the inner ward," I said, trying to impress Jeremy with my knowledge. "The moat is dried up, though. The walls of the keep are in quite good condition. The drawbridge is rotted in places, but it's still quite safe."

"Wonderful!" Jeremy enthused. He stopped and took out his handkerchief again – rather grubby by this time – and patted the back of his neck. The sun was high and it was quite hot. "Where are we going to have our picnic? I'm sure looking forward to it!"

"Come on!" I called to Thomas. "We're starving!"

He sauntered over, still looking rather sullen. "I'm going inside," he said, starting over the drawbridge. From his shoulder Betty turned and called, "Aow, aow."

"Then I guess we'd better follow," said Jeremy. The massive gates on the other side of the drawbridge were still in place – not that they looked as if they would ever again be able to be closed against intruders. Their huge hinges were crumbling with layers of rust. They drooped sadly, as if knowing that their days of usefulness were long over.

"Pity your Mom and Dad couldn't have joined us," Jeremy said suddenly. "Sounds like this ... ah ... writing keeps them awful busy?"

"Yes," I said, wondering if this was a trick question.

"Don't they ever take time off?" he persisted.

"Um ... not often," I murmured.

"It must be very important work." He gave me a quick glance.

"It is. I ... I mean ... they've got deadlines and things."

"So. They let you two go off all over the island, by yourselves, hmm?"

"Well ... usually we do lessons in the mornings. But in the afternoons, we..."

"Don't they ever worry about you? Wandering all over the place – without someone looking after you?"

I felt a cold prickle of fear up the back of my neck. The way he had said "without someone looking after you" sounded so menacing. "It's ... very ... safe," I began. "I mean ... it's not like back on the mainland..."

"But there must be dangers of a different sort, here," he said slowly. I glanced up and caught his eye. He seemed to be staring at me.

"We're ... we can look after ourselves," I finished lamely.

We were walking under the portcullis, our footsteps sounding loud and lonely on the ancient cobblestones. The prickle of fear crept all over my scalp. Thomas and I could be walking further and further into a trap. But what sort? And why?

And then the plot suddenly dawned on me. If Jeremy was a spy, working for some enemy organization, this would be the perfect chance for him to tie us up and hold us captive until our parents agreed to give up the secrets of our organization. I could see instantly how it would all fit. I looked at Jeremy with new suspicious insight. I must tell Thomas. I had to let him know I'd worked it out. But where was he?

"This looks like a good spot." Jeremy sat down against the wall in the sun, facing the castle. "Where's that brother of yours?" He opened his lunch. "Can't wait for him, I'm afraid – too hungry," he mumbled, speaking with his mouth full, I noticed.

I was about to say I'd go and look for Thomas when I remembered his instructions to keep my eyes peeled. I'd better stay here and watch Jeremy. I sat down and opened my lunch bag. At first I thought I couldn't eat a crumb – I was too nervous. But then I thought I'd better eat. Just in case Jeremy did tie us up … just in case this was the last meal I'd get for a long time. When I smelt the food I realized I was really hungry. The filled rolls were great. I wolfed down one and then another, then ate a hard-boiled egg more slowly and finally munched through an apple. It was very quiet and hot against the wall. I began to feel sleepy.

Jeremy hadn't said much, except the occasional grunt of appreciation over the food.

Mum had given him cans of drink for all of us. He asked me what I wanted and opened a can of Coke and passed it over. I drank a large mouthful and began to feel very sleepy. Perhaps it was only the heat and the food, but I longed to close my eyes, just for a few minutes.

"Think I might just have a little snooze," said Jeremy, echoing my longing. "Hope you don't mind? I'm feeling rather sleepy." He slid down into the grass and put his sweater over his face. "Wake me up when we're ready to go."

I felt so sleepy that if I'd had Thomas's suspicious mind, I'd have believed I was drugged. I must try to keep awake ... I must ... I must...

The next thing I knew was the stifling feeling of a heavy weight on my chest. I couldn't breathe. Something was covering my nose and scraping my face – something thick and rough.

"Polly – Polly – wake up!" a voice shouted.

The world went red. I opened my eyes to dazzling light, my heart pounding with fear.

"What's the matter?" I asked, terrified.

And then I realized that the heavy weight on my chest was only Betty, who had been licking my face as if trying to give me the kiss of life. I pushed her off and sat up.

"Oh, Pol!" Thomas sank down into the grass, his face white. "I thought you were dead! You looked so – so – still and ... dead. I thought..." He looked around. "Where *is* Jeremy, anyway?"

"You thought he'd killed me?"

He gave a long, shuddering sigh. "Yes. I was really frightened!" We looked at each other seriously and then both burst out laughing. "Don't you ever frighten me that way again!" he said, when he was able talk.

"Me?" I suddenly felt more cheerful than I had all day. "It was all in your mind – nothing to do with me at all!"

"Wow!" He leaned back against the wall. "All shook up! Honest, Polly – I really did think you were dead."

"So did Betty. It's a wonder I've got any skin left!" My face felt quite tender where Betty had licked it. "Oh, bother! I was trying so hard to stay awake. Jeremy decided to have a sleep, but I was determined to stay awake. He was just there." I pointed to a squashed patch in the grass. "I wonder how long I was asleep. Where did you get to, anyway? You disappeared completely, the moment we got over the drawbridge!"

"Just thought I'd keep a watch on you from above," said Thomas, sounding mysterious. "I saw you eating your lunch and him go to sleep – or pretend to! Then I saw you drop off and I thought I'd better get back, so while I was coming down he must have woken up and left. You looked so white and still. I was sure he'd done something to you while I wasn't looking, but…" His voice trailed off and then he began again. "Maybe we're wrong, Pol. He hasn't really done anything nasty – in fact, he's been rather nice, really."

"I know. That's what I was thinking all the time," I broke in, "except – now I've worked it out!"

"What do you mean?"

"There didn't really seem to be anything he could do, if he was working for the enemy. I mean, what is the point of doing anything to two kids? Mum's always telling us that huge organizations are involved in the conservation battle, so why spend time on two kids? Except –" I lowered my voice, looking around to make sure Jeremy wasn't in sight – "I've worked out what the reason could be!"

"What?" Thomas was impatient.

"If he held us captive, he could make demands on Mum and Dad for our release. He could—"

"Blackmail them! Demand that they cease working for the organization – or give away important secrets – or destroy data bases ... all sorts of stuff!" Light dawned on Thomas. "Of course. That makes absolute sense!" He looked at me with admiration. "Brilliant, Pol! That has to be the motive!"

"Mind you, Tommo, he's only here by accident. And it was Mum's idea that we should go off with him today. I don't suppose he'd have suggested it. And he hasn't shown any signs of being the enemy, not really."

"Not yet!" said Thomas grimly. "There's still time! I don't think we should spend any longer here than we need to." He looked at his watch. "Anyway, it's time to go."

"Just what I thought," said a cheerful voice, making us jump. Where had he sprung from?

"Phew! You're always doing that," said Thomas, pretending to smile. "You must be able to walk through walls!"

"Aha!" Jeremy smiled enigmatically. "Who knows? Plenty of walls to walk through around here, anyway. Hope you didn't mind me slipping off and leaving you," he added. "Thought I'd pop off and do a little exploring. You looked so peaceful – didn't have the heart to wake you."

"Sorry, I went to sleep." I felt a start of fear at the thought that he had looked at me in such a vulnerable state. "I didn't realize how tired I was. We should go now, though," I said, turning to Thomas urgently. I suddenly just wanted to get out of the place.

We wound down the zigzag walk and around the bottom of the motte, towards the beach. Betty was leaping about with excited squeaks of pleasure. She knew we were heading for the beach, her favourite walk. The path was well marked and Jeremy led the way, turning every now and then to beckon us on. Somewhere along the way he had assumed his

natural adult position of leadership. Tommo
and I walked together behind him, feeling
increasingly resentful.

"Who does he think he is!" muttered
Thomas. "Just because he's older than us.
You'd think it was *his* island!"

"Perhaps he's just anxious to get back.
Doesn't want to miss the helicopter?" I
suggested.

"Rubbish. He's just naturally bossy! We
should be leading the way, not him. How do
we know he won't lead us into some sort of
trap?"

I sighed. "I wish I could make up my mind
whether he's the enemy or not. Why d'you
think Mum was suspicious of him?"

"She has to be suspicious of anyone. I mean
– even if he wasn't the enemy, we'd have to be
careful he didn't find out what we're up to.
You know that. Once word gets out, our usefulness is over."

"Mmm." I kicked at a stone. "He's quite
nice, you know," I said slowly, knowing
Thomas would disagree with me. "He hasn't
actually done anything nasty yet – not really. I
think he's trying to be friendly. I hate having
to be suspicious and careful all the time. I hope
he's not the enemy. I like him."

"That's the trouble with you," Thomas said
with disgust. "You always get soppy – let your
emotions get the better of you!"

That was it. I was fed up with Thomas being so rude, especially when I'd come up with so many good ideas all day! I turned away and marched on ahead of him, "Shove off!" I called over my shoulder, walking faster.

"Don't be such an idiot!" he yelled. I walked on without replying. "Polly – Polly!" he yelled again, but I wouldn't turn around.

Jeremy was watching, and just at the wrong time he beckoned with an irritating, bossy gesture. I deliberately slowed down. Thomas saw and grinned. He called in a friendlier tone, "Pol – wait a bit." I stopped and waited for him to catch up. "Suppose we just disappear and go back home another way? He'd be all right. He couldn't miss the lighthouse from here."

I was just about to agree to Thomas's suggestion when Jeremy called, suddenly and urgently, beckoning to us from the top of the cliff. Betty jumped up and nipped at Thomas's fingers, miaowing impatiently, begging him to follow Jeremy.

"Look at him!" grumbled Thomas. "You'd think he was the flipping headmaster..."

"Shhh, Thomas!" I could see Jeremy was upset. "I think there's something the matter." I started running towards him, beginning also to be aware of a strange, alarming noise from the beach. Thomas followed me.

"Look – look!" Jeremy was shouting,

pointing to the beach, as I reached the top of the cliff. I screamed with horror. It was a terrible sight. The beach was crowded with adult seals who had all come onto land to have their calves. But instead of contented families of mothers and babies, guarded by the big bull seals, all basking on the rocks and diving and playing happily in the sea, the beach was stained with blood. A few dead baby seals were scattered among rocks and sand, their white fur stained red – but only a few. Anyone who knew the seal colony could see that most of the babies had been slaughtered and stolen. The cries from the mothers and fathers were heartbreaking. Their huge, beautiful eyes looked up to the sky as they rolled their heads from side to side, moaning and crying and bellowing, nuzzling each other.

Thomas arrived, out of breath. "Oh, no!" he gasped. "They've been murdered ... the baby seals ... *oh no!*" He grabbed me and forced my head against his shoulder. "*Don't look!*" he yelled.

But it was too late. I had seen it all. Betty was whimpering and backing away from the edge of the cliff.

"Betty – Betty – come on," he called, and grabbing my hand he turned and pulled me down the path, away from the awful scene. Betty followed. We ran as fast as we could towards the lighthouse.

CHAPTER ELEVEN

We were both gasping for air, with the agony of stitches in our sides, when we limped up to the lighthouse. Thomas yelled loudly as we came up to the door, "Dad – Dad – Dad…" Dad flew out, followed immediately by Mum. "What on earth…?" he began, and then his words were drowned out by a throbbing in the sky. I scooped up Betty, who had valiantly kept up with us all the way but who was now about to run away in panic, her tail like a bottle-brush. I hugged her tightly, trying to calm her frantic wriggling. A violent wind swept over our heads; the throbbing grew louder and suddenly a helicopter was hovering overhead, about to land. Dad kept looking at us curiously. He could see from our faces that something terrible had happened, but there was no chance to discuss it. He shrugged and waved us inside. Mum followed us in.

I dropped Betty and began to blurt out, "Oh, Mum – the babies … murdered … blood everywhere … it was so awful!"

I wasn't making much sense and Mum was looking confused.

Thomas interrupted, "Polly – let me – we haven't much time – Jeremy will be back in a moment…"

"What is it – what is it? What's happened?" Mum was obviously shocked at the sight of our red, sweaty faces and scratched arms and legs.

"The baby seals have been slaughtered! It's horrible. Blood all over the beach – the adult seals are screaming—"

"Jeremy discovered it!" I whispered, bending over and trying to ease the stitch in my side.

"Well, we would have. He was just first!" snapped Thomas.

Mum gave a gasp. "Oh, no! Not the baby seals!" She looked at us, her face twisted with sadness. "What did Jeremy say?"

We looked at each other, not understanding what she was getting at.

"How did he seem to react?" Mum suddenly looked stern.

"Well…" Thomas paused, trying to think.

"We ran away," I said. "It was so dreadful. We just looked for a moment and then ran and ran…"

"Did he look upset?" Mum pressed.

"Ye–es. I think so ... at least, he called us to come and look..."

"He did look upset," Thomas interrupted, "but he could have just been putting it on – pretending..."

Mum spoke urgently. "Doesn't matter now. He'll be here soon. He won't be far behind. Now, listen. Both of you! You mustn't look quite so upset when he arrives. Pretend you're sad, but that you're not too worried – it's just one of the unpleasant facts of life."

"Why?" She must be joking. "Why should we pretend? He won't believe us. No one could see that sight and not be horrified."

"Polly – you must give the impression that it doesn't mean anything special to you, just as most people don't care about parrots or monkeys being taken from the wild. Don't you see? That's the only way we can be of any use. Once people begin to suspect what we're doing here, we've had it!" She looked at us fiercely. "Can you both do that?"

We nodded glumly.

"I know it's not easy, but there's too much at stake. Anyway, it won't be for long. He'll be gone very soon."

"What are you going to do – about the seals?" asked Thomas.

"Your father and I will have to investigate as soon as we can. I can't understand why we

104

didn't detect it from the lighthouse. It must have happened early this morning, and I guess, after the day we had yesterday, we weren't on full alert. Maybe the hunters were in the caves, where the seals shelter. It just goes to show how terrible things can happen right under your nose!" She shuddered. "We've got to try and get those hunters. They are vile."

Outside, the throbbing of the helicopter had slowed down and stopped. We could hear Dad greeting the pilot and then Jeremy's voice, talking loudly.

"Mum went to the door. "Hullo Jeremy. You got back all right then," she said cheerily, and went out.

"Come on, Pol. Let's go and pretend," Thomas said gloomily.

"I want to go up and see Squawkette," I said, really thinking I couldn't face Jeremy any more.

"Wait until he's gone," said Thomas. "You know he'll only come in to say goodbye, and stuff. Let's get it over and done with."

"Oh ... OK," I agreed, reluctantly, and we went outside.

Jeremy was telling Mum and Dad and the pilot all about the seal slaughter. They were all shaking their heads sadly. Dad was saying what a pity it was and how awful people were – all the usual sort of clichés people spout when they can't really be bothered to think about unpleasant things. Mum was murmuring the same sort of words. The pilot looked more upset than they did, but he kept looking at his watch.

"Look, I hate to interrupt," he said, finally, "but we've got to get going. Only a few more hours of good daylight. I want to get you back to the mainland well before dark."

Jeremy sighed. "Uh-huh. OK. I've just got to gather a few things, and then we're outta here!" He turned towards the lighthouse and saw us. "Hi, you two," he said with a funny look. "Beat me back, then? Wondered where you went!"

"Sorry we didn't wait for you," Thomas stammered. "Thing is – we didn't like the look of that beach. Thought it wasn't really the place for a walk." He even managed a sort of laugh.

"Sure wasn't!" Jeremy looked strained. "Terrible sight. Terrible!" He shook his head and pursed his mouth, blowing air out in a long, mournful whistle. "Don't care if I never see such a sight again in my whole life! Sorry you had to see it, little Polly Pickford," he said sadly, putting his arm around me.

"Oh, well," I said in a quavery voice, trying to make it sound sort of careless. "I guess I'll survive."

"Uh-huh." He looked at me thoughtfully. "Ata girl! Never thank you enough for what

106

you did for me yesterday – both of you. And your parents, of course." He reached out his hand to Thomas. "Best of luck, Tommo."

Thomas shook hands with him, murmuring, "And you."

"Bye, Polly." Jeremy shook my hand. "Keep up the good work!"

"Bye, Jeremy," I said with relief, "And we can never thank you enough for saving Squawkette."

"Oh, I'll say," said Thomas, and I could see he felt guilty for forgetting. Today's happenings had made him quite forget yesterday's.

"Well, kinda funny how things turn out. I guess it was just good luck," said Jeremy.

Meanwhile, Mum had gone into the lighthouse again and came out lugging a duffle bag. "I think this was all you had," she said, handing it over.

"Oh – that's kind of you." Jeremy looked at it. "All that's left of my adventure!" he said with a dejected shrug. "Bye, everyone!" He gave a salute and turned towards the helicopter.

I suddenly felt really sad for him. He looked sort of forlorn, as if he wanted to stay. "I hope he's not the enemy," I whispered again to Thomas as we watched him climb into the plane.

"You can be very boring at times, Pol," he said grumpily.

*   *   *

We were still waving goodbye with silly, broad smiles pasted on our faces, when Dad shouted through the noise of the helicopter, "Come on – we've got to get down to that beach to see what's going on with all those seals!"

"Right!" yelled Thomas and we all ran into the lighthouse to get ready.

"Hold on!" said Dad as we panted into the kitchen. "You and Polly are staying here."

"Oh, Dad. No!" said Thomas pleadingly.

"Yes – I mean it." When Dad looked like that, we knew he wouldn't change his mind.

"For one thing," Mum said, "you're both far too tired. You've walked miles already today and you both look as if you could drop!"

"I'm all right," said Thomas indignantly. "Just because Polly's looking a bit scruffy." He gave me a dismissive glance. For once I didn't protest, because to tell the truth I couldn't bear the thought of going back to that ghastly scene.

"It could be dangerous," Dad continued. "Someone has to stay here to take messages…"

"Please, Dad – let me go with you. Mum and Polly can stay here."

"No. Sorry, Thomas. Not this time. I need someone fresh and alert. You're exhausted. I can see it. You'd only hold me up."

Thomas stopped protesting. He could see

108

the sense in that. "OK," he said reluctantly, and slumped in a chair.

"But don't think you can just sit there," Dad said. "Come upstairs. I need you to man the communications room – both of you."

"Hurry!" Mum called as we went up.

I hadn't realized just how tired I was until I walked up the stairs. Each foot felt like a lead weight. As Dad showed us what to do I could hardly concentrate. It wasn't anything very new. He just went through the routine with us once again to make sure we knew exactly what we were doing.

"Now. Make sure you get supper – feed Betty and Squawkette. And don't worry," said Mum as they waved goodbye.

"We should be home by about midnight. But if we're any later, take it in turns to sleep in the communications room, in case we need to get in touch," Dad instructed.

"Tommo – make yourself a large cup of strong coffee," Mum said. Then, seeing how tired I looked, "Perhaps you should have a sleep now, and relieve Tommo after supper? Bye, darlings." She kissed us both.

"Keep alert!" called Dad, "We need you!" And they were gone.

"I'm really exhausted. I think I will have a sleep for a couple of hours," I said after the door slammed. I expected Thomas to say something about how hopeless girls were, but he looked quite sympathetic.

"Go on, then," he said. "I'll wake you at about nine."

I fell into bed with Betty gratefully snuggling up to me and knew nothing until I felt Thomas shaking me, hours later. I struggled to open my eyes.

"Time to get up, Pol," he said, yawning. "I'm about ready for a kip – but I'm starving. Want to man the communications room or make supper?"

"I think I'll make supper," I said glumly, not wanting Thomas to choose mine for me. I went groggily down to the storeroom and wandered around looking at the different packs of frozen meals until after a while I started to feel hungry. I decided on chicken and mushroom casserole, new potatoes and asparagus with garlic butter for me, a huge pizza with chips for Thomas and chocolate ice-cream for both of us. As I slid the packs over the reorder scanner, I began to think about Mum and Dad. What were they doing right at this moment? I imagined them out there in the darkness, probably cold and hungry by now. Maybe they were in danger? I wished they were safely at home.

I went up to the kitchen, cooked the food and took it all up to the communications room on a tray. Thomas looked at my first course with disgust.

"Yuk! You choose such revolting meals," he said.

"Just think yourself lucky I let you have what you want," I said glaring at him.

We finished supper and I took over in the communications room while Thomas stacked the dishwasher and then went for a sleep. "Wake me at midnight, Pol," he called as he went upstairs. "Or whenever. Don't let me sleep through anything exciting!"

"OK – OK," I called after him, and then I was alone, and for a moment I noticed how, like it says in that poem "The Listeners", by Walter de la Mare, *the silence surged softly backwards* when the sound of his footsteps were gone.

CHAPTER TWELVE

It was lonely in the communications room. I'd never been in there all by myself before. The room was mostly in darkness and the monitor screens could be seen clearly above glowing pools of light from spotlights shining on the keyboards. The shadows in the corners of the room were ominous. I sat on a stool at the control panel and checked the various messages and weather reports that had come in. The light was above me but the shadows were all around. Despite the flickering screens and the hum and buzz and blips and squeaks of hundreds of people communicating in various ways over thousands of miles, I felt even more lonely than if I were walking along the beach by myself.

It was funny – there were people at the other end of the messages that curled out of the fax machine or flickered on the computer and satellite screens – but it didn't feel like people. Dad was always telling us that technology was only a tool: humans were the important part.

"Your mind is a virtual reality machine," he often said. "You can go anywhere you want in your head – without the aid of technology. It's up to you to create your own VR environment. But to get to the most exciting places, you have to programme your brain properly. You'll never be bored if you input knowledge and wisdom. Information is not enough."

One day I'd asked him what he meant. "What's the difference between information and knowledge? And what's wisdom, then?"

"Information is mostly facts," he began. "Like how much things cost or who won the World Cup or how many of Henry VIII's wives were beheaded. For example, the phone book is full of information. But it's a boring read. See what I mean?"

I nodded. "Yes. The Net is full of it."

"Sure is," Dad said. "But knowledge is more interesting – it's understanding how the facts came to be. If you know about Henry VIII, you'll know which wives were beheaded and why. That's more interesting than how many."

"Oh, yes." I could see that straight away.

"And wisdom is the most interesting of all. It's understanding which of the facts and knowledge is true and which is lies – and why

113

this is important. Get it?"

"Mmm. I think so," I'd said.

"Wisdom takes the longest and it's the hardest to find," he'd said. "But if you look for it, Pol, you'll get it in the end."

I thought about that now, and wondered exactly what he'd meant. Dad said a lot of things I didn't quite understand – and yet, I sort of did. Mum loved to read us poetry; that's why a line from a poem often came into my head, like the thought I'd had when Thomas went up to bed, about the silence surging softly backwards. I began thinking about the poem – it's scary – about phantom listeners in a lonely house, listening in the moonlight to a traveller knocking on the door … just listening and not answering … and I felt the hair on the back of my neck begin to prickle…

"Oh, stop it!" I snapped, giving myself a shake. If I went on like this I'd be a mess in no time. Where was Mum now, and Dad? Were they all right? I wished Thomas was awake. Betty came into the room and jumped up on the other chair, with a little "miaow." I was really glad to see her. I stroked her silky coat while she purred and after a while she fell asleep.

I watched the radar beam scanning the area, showing the distinctive shape of the island coastline and other familiar marks every time

114

it swung around the screen. The marks were called "contacts" because they showed up every time the radar beam contacted them. I noticed a new contact moving closer and closer to the coastline. Was it a ship or was it just an extra-large wave – sea clutter?

I reached over to the control panel and tried to get a better picture, adjusting the brilliance, gain, range and tuning knobs in turn. The contact remained steady and clear. It must be a ship, perhaps heading towards the beach where the seals were. The beach was too far underneath the headland to be detected. I could see why Mum and Dad wouldn't have been able to see the seal slaughter happening almost under their noses.

I knew I should work out the exact direction of the ship and how quickly it was moving. I pulled the pad of plotting sheets towards me and each time the beam swept around again, marked a cross on the sheet at exactly the same spot as on the screen. Yes, the ship was about three and a half miles away, travelling at about eleven knots, heading for the headland on one side of the beach, too far away yet for Mum and Dad to see it. Who was it and what were they up to? I'd have to warn Mum and Dad. I thought carefully: Dad had his mobile and his personal pager on him. He'd told us not to call him on the mobile – he'd have turned it off, anyway, because the ringing of the phone could give them away.

"Don't even use the pager unless absolutely necessary," he'd said. "We'll contact you when we need to."

Was this absolutely necessary? I wished Thomas were here to ask, but I couldn't wait that long. I had to make a decision now. I'd send Dad a message on the pager. Just one small bleep and the words would appear on the little display panel. That would be best.

I sat down at the main computer keyboard and pressed P for pager:

SHIP APPROACHING BEACH THREE MILES AWAY TRAVELLING ELEVEN KNOTS I typed onto the screen, but the message was too long. I wasn't very good at short messages. I racked my brains and tried again: SHIP 3 MILES AWAY COMING 11 KNOTS. Yes, that was better. Then I pressed Exit/Send and the message flashed on and off telling me that the bleeper on the pager at the other end had bleeped and the message was appearing. OK TRANSMIT appeared on the screen. I sighed with relief. At least now Mum and Dad would be warned. I checked the radar screen to see how close the mystery ship had come. They were probably within viewing distance of the lighthouse by now.

On the wall behind the control panel was a window looking out at just that part of the ocean where the ship would appear. I looked

116

and couldn't see anything but blackness. I checked the radar again. The ship was getting closer to the beach but I still couldn't see it through the window. The radar showed that it was very close. Why couldn't I see any sign of it through the window? Then it occurred to me that it mustn't be using lights. That could mean only one thing: it must be dodgy. It's terribly dangerous to travel without lights, both for other vessels and for your own ship. Only pirate ships or illegal operators dare to. As the contact on the radar screen moved closer and closer to the shoreline, I just kept looking into the blackness – and finally saw a bright flash of light, offshore – and then another. And then I saw something that sent a chill of fear right through me: an answering beam of light flashed from the shore. Someone was waiting on the beach for the approaching ship. Who was it? And where were Mum and Dad?

I ran upstairs, shouting to Thomas to wake up. He was already sitting up in bed looking startled when I burst through the door.

"What's the matter?" he said.

"There's a ship out in the bay, signalling to the shore. And someone on the shore is signalling back – and I've warned Dad, but I haven't had any answer."

He looked at me for a long moment and then at his watch. "Nearly midnight," he said, jumping out of bed, pulling a sweater on.

"And you haven't heard anything from Mum and Dad?" he asked, as his head struggled through the sweater.

"No – nothing. I'm worried!"

"Mum and Dad said we weren't to worry. They said exactly that!" he snapped as we ran down to the communications room.

"I can't help it," I said miserably, "I just feel that something is wrong."

"OK." He sat down in front of the radar. "Is that the ship?" He pointed to a contact on the screen.

"Yes – at least I think so. I would have thought they'd have gone further into the shore, behind the headland, to avoid detection, but..."

"They're not expecting detection. They don't know the lighthouse is manned," Thomas snapped again. "At least, they won't know if you haven't given the game away!"

"How could I? I've been really careful," I said furiously.

"How did you warn Dad?"

"I just paged him. He said it would be too dangerous to phone. Besides, he's switched his mobile phone off."

"Good." Thomas sat down in front of the computer keyboard and downloaded the pager message. OK TRANSMIT appeared beside the message.

He stared at me, frowning. "Either he never

received it, or he couldn't confirm," he said slowly. He looked out the window. There was nothing to be seen, nothing but the moon beginning to come up over the sea. "Look how bright it is," he said, pointing to it. "That's not going to do anyone any good. It'll only make the crew on the ship more careful."

"Tommo," I said slowly, "If Dad didn't receive the message, it can only be because … because … he's lost the pager … or he's had an accident … or …"

"…they've been captured," finished Thomas. "OK, but for goodness' sake, let's keep calm."

We stared at each other, hating what we were thinking, frightened to speak our fears but unable to pretend things were all right. Horrible hot fever began churning through my stomach. "We've got to go and see what's happening," I said at last. "We've got to!"

"But Mum said we were not to worry. She said it specially – just as they were leaving. They didn't expect to be home before midnight. It's only quarter past now."

"I don't care. I'm going even if you're not!" I ran out. I couldn't just sit there doing nothing.

Thomas followed. "Pol – Pol!" he yelled, catching up with me on the stairs. "We've got to have a plan! It's no good just rushing off."

We sat on the stairs. "We've got to take stuff – food and things – in case they've had an accident," I said.

"Yes," Thomas agreed. "Bandages – torches – brandy…"

"Brandy's no good. It only makes people worse if they're in shock," I said, remembering a programme I'd seen on TV about accidents.

"Yes – but they may be exposed – you know, like people are on mountains. Those dogs always bring brandy," Thomas insisted.

I couldn't be bothered to argue. "OK, then. But only if we have a small bottle." I stood up. "I'm going to get a sweater and coat. Oh – and I'll heat some soup – put it in a Thermos."

Thomas had a brainwave. "Perhaps I should send a message to HQ?"

"Oh – of course!" I didn't say so, but I was shocked that I hadn't thought of it. Dad had showed us how to do that only a couple of days ago. He'd said we might need to know how, in extreme emergencies. Was it an extreme emergency now? If Thomas thought so, it must be. "Good thinking," I said, miserably. I was discovering how much I hated extreme emergencies. "Look, you send the message while I get the other things. Oh – and feed Squawkette. Make sure she's got plenty of food – in case … in case…" I couldn't finish the sentence, but Thomas knew what I meant. In case we didn't get back tonight.

CHAPTER THIRTEEN

I finally decided on chicken soup – I remembered people had that when they were sick –
and a small bottle of brandy to keep Thomas
happy. Then because the backpack was getting
rather heavy with the bandages, a towel,
torches and some apples, I slipped a large bar
of chocolate into one of the deep pockets of my
coat.

As we set off, the moon was huge. We knew
the path well, anyway, but in the bright moonlight it was almost as easy to follow as in the
day. We'd been walking for about a quarter of
an hour when we heard a pattering of little
feet, and Betty appeared.

"Oh, Thomas!" I was furious. "I thought
you'd shut the cat-flap!"

"Oh, no!" Thomas looked at Betty angrily.
"She's obviously been following us all the
way."

"Aow!" Betty said in agreement, rubbing up against him and then smarming all over me.

"Betty – you're really bad!" he growled. "You know you're not allowed out after dark. And it might be dangerous!"

"Aow!" she returned cheekily, sticking her nose in the air and quite plainly saying she didn't care.

"It's too late to go back now. Betty!" I glared at her. She stared back, eyes big and intelligent. "If we're in danger, you'll have to jump up a tree, or something."

"Uh! Oh!" said Betty, and with a flick of her tail she bobbed happily up the path ahead of us.

We went along the cliffs for about a mile until we came to the headland overlooking the beach. On the top of the headland was a large crop of rock. We crept up behind it and peered over the edge, onto the beach below. The tide had washed the beach clean and now the sand glimmered palely in the moonlight. The castle looked sternly down at the murder scene. The rocks tumbling down from the headland, ringing the edge of the bay, were dark, brooding shadows. There were no seals to be seen. When they were ashore, they spent most of their time in the caves under the headland on which we were standing. There was no ship, no dinghy, no sign of Mum and Dad. Nothing to be seen, except the familiar beach and rocks.

"Where's the mystery ship?" I whispered, looking from the beach to the horizon. "It's vanished. It's just nowhere to be seen."

"Probably gone around to the other side of the far headland," said Thomas quietly. "If that's the case, they must have a reason. And the reason must be…"

"Us?"

Thomas looked at me grimly. "What else? They wouldn't be hiding like this if they thought they were undetected."

"They must have come back tonight for a reason," I said, thinking it through. "Perhaps to collect something…?"

"Or someone."

"Maybe the boat drops off the hunters and then comes back and collects them after they've done their dreadful deed?"

"Makes sense," Thomas agreed. "And the fact that they're hiding now, instead of just heading out to sea again, means they know something's up."

"Oh, Tommo!" I grabbed his arm. "That means Mum and Dad have been seen … or … captured."

"Don't jump to conclusions," said Thomas gruffly, but already I was thinking that perhaps capture was the least terrible possibility. "Maybe there's a simple reason – one we haven't thought of," he said, trying to be cheerful. I looked at him, wondering what he was really thinking. It was too awful to say what was in my mind, so I said nothing.

"Look, Pol – d'you want to go back and wait until HQ sends help?"

"No! No!" That was a dreadful idea. "It'll take ages for them to arrive. We've got to do something now!" Betty, who had been walking around the rocks, leaned down from a high one and gave me a gentle kiss and then jumped into down into my arms. I hugged her fiercely, trying to block out my frightening thoughts. "What are we going to do, Tommo – what's the plan?"

"I think the first place we should head for is the large cave underneath here," he said slowly. "That's the most likely place for Mum and Dad to hide. But we'll go the secret way."

Only we knew this route into the large cave. We'd discovered it one day when we'd seen a seal suddenly emerge from underneath a bush near the top of the cliff. It was a narrow tunnel with a series of torturous, wet, slippery slopes and steps, twisting and turning down into the cave. I gritted my teeth. I didn't like it much in the daylight. Right now, I couldn't think of anything I wanted to do less.

"OK," I agreed glumly. "But I do wish there was another way."

"So do I," said Thomas.

"I'll never get down the tunnel with this backpack," I said, hoping to change his mind.

"Too bad. Leave it."

"Betty might get lost," I said, finally.

"You're joking! It's exactly her sort of territory," he said scornfully. "Come on. I'll lead the way."

We scrambled away from the cliff edge, heading towards the hidden hole.

"Have you got your torch, Pol?" Thomas asked as he pushed aside the branches and shone a beam of light down into the depths of the dark tunnel. It looked so secretive and sly, so capable of closing over us – and burying us alive.

"Yes," I sighed.

"Right!" he said, and began the descent.

CHAPTER FOURTEEN

Down and down we squirmed, slithering and scrambling, sometimes using our elbows to brace ourselves against the cold, slimy walls of the tunnel, sometimes sliding too fast, sometimes having to squeeze around corners and all the time trying to be as quiet as possible. Betty followed behind me, enjoying it all thoroughly. She kept patting me on the head from time to time, trying to turn it into a game of tag.

I had to fight that awful feeling of being buried alive. It was hard to breathe, but if I gave way to panic and tried to struggle it would get worse. I forced myself to keep calm and think of Mum and Dad and how they needed us, and that it would soon be over. It was a help to be able to see the faint glow of Thomas's torch and the top of his head. He knew how much I hated confined spaces so he helped as much as possible, telling me I was doing well and that we were nearly there.

"Won't be long, Pol," he kept saying, "Just keep going. Try not to think about it."

After what seemed like hours, the tunnel began to widen and we knew we were close to the end. At last I heard Thomas drop onto the floor of the cave.

"I'm down, Pol," he called, and in a few seconds I was beside him.

"Thank goodness that's over!" I shuddered.

"Turn your torch off," he whispered, and suddenly we were in what seemed like complete blackness. We waited until our eyes got used to the dark, and after a while could see a faint glimmer coming from one direction, so we knew that was the way to go.

"Where's Betty?" Thomas asked.

Immediately a small mew came from behind him.

"Shhh Betty – quiet," he whispered. "Are you ready, Pol?"

"Yes," I whispered.

"Hold my hand," he murmured as we crept forward, "and be very careful where you step. Feel the way with your toe first. Don't go tripping over anything."

We were as quiet as possible – so quiet that even our breathing sounded loud. I was getting more and more nervous – and then suddenly I heard something.

"Shhh." I grabbed Thomas's arm. "Did you hear that?"

We both stood absolutely still.

"Maybe it was just a seal," I whispered after a while. "It sounded like a man's cough, but..."

And then we both heard it again. A harsh, hacking cough, followed by a rough voice which sounded as if it was swearing furiously.

"Can't ya shut that cough up?" we heard the voice complain. "Nothin' but cough, cough, cough – I'm sick of it!"

There was another cough.

"Ah – for cryin' out loud," grumbled the other. Then there was silence for a while.

"Aow! Aow!" said Betty suddenly, and jumped up onto a ledge above our heads. We froze with horror. It sounded so loud, we were sure the men would hear it. Thomas picked Betty up and held her tightly and we pressed ourselves against the cave wall with hearts thumping. "They can't hear us as well as we can hear them," I realized. "The noise of the sea is louder at the cave mouth."

"Of course!" Thomas breathed a sigh of relief and put Betty back on the ledge. We crept forward again. The cave was getting lighter and the noise of the sea was getting louder. We knew we were close to the mouth. The men must be sitting there.

Not far from the entrance, the cave turned

a corner. We crept right up to it and then stopped. We could hear the men quite clearly now.

"They're takin' their time about it," one of them was saying. "Thought they'd be 'ere by now."

"Maybe there's only one of 'em – can't leave the lighthouse unattended," said the other.

Thomas nudged me. The men were talking about us!

"Well, there can't be all that many of 'em," continued the first man. "Not a whole gang of 'em, anyway. Not enough room in that lighthouse."

"Could be two or three. We'll handle 'em, though."

There was a silence for a while. "Must be a couple of hours since they sent that message?" said the first man after a while.

"What the hell are they doin' on that lighthouse, anyway? Lighthouse's been unmanned for years, now. Don't make no sense!"

"Well, this one's goin' to be unmanned soon, an' all!" said the first with a cruel laugh. "Soon as they come creepin' out – we'll unman 'em!" He began to cough harshly again.

Under cover of the loud coughing, Thomas crept forward and peered around the corner. As he turned back to me I could see his eyes, huge with terror. "It's the hunters, all right! There's a whole stack of baby seal skins piled up beside them. And they've got guns," he whispered. "Rifles!" He grabbed my arm and we peered at each other in the gloom. "We've got to get rid of them if we can – throw the guns away – into the sea!"

"No ... no, Thomas!" I whispered, desperately afraid he'd do something stupid.

"Shhh!" He put a finger on my mouth and, signalling to me to stay where I was, crept forward to peer round the corner again.

Suddenly Betty, who had been sitting on the ledge, jumped down and ran madly around the corner, towards the light. I nearly screamed, but I clapped my hand over my mouth just in time. Thomas turned and looked at me, his mouth open in a silent scream of horror. There was nothing we could do. I could hardly bear to see what was going to happen – but I simply had to. I crept up to the corner and peered around it and let out an "eek" of fear.

"Shhh!" Thomas whispered, jabbing me sharply with his elbow while I dug my fingers into his arm. "Pol – you're hurting!" he murmured. But I couldn't help it!

The men were sitting at the entrance, slumped against one wall of the cave. We could see them quite clearly in the bright moonlight. Betty scampered up to them, sideways, her tail highly arched, the fur sticking out like a bottle-brush. It was her fear sign: fear and challenge. We'd seen her take on huge dogs like this, and win!

"Bloody hell!" we heard one of the men shout. "It's that sodding cat again!"

"The one that followed us yesterday? The one we threw in the lake? How did it get here?"

"Must have got outta that sack! You didn't tie it proper!

"Nah – I tied it real tight! Must be a sodding ghost!" shouted the other.

"Should'a wrung its neck … aagh!" the man suddenly yelled as Betty leapt up at him on all four legs, slashed his face with her needle-sharp claws, bounced off and streaked out of the cave.

"What the…!" he screamed with shock. Dark scratches appeared on his face and popped with blood. "Get the sodding thing! Put a bullet through its brain!" he yelled, and rubbed his face with his sleeve while the other man leapt up with his gun and ran after Betty.

Now we really were scared. I closed my eyes and buried my face in Thomas's shoulder.

"She'll be all right, Pol – I'm sure she'll be!" he whispered.

After a few minutes the injured man began to mumble. "Bloody fool," he said angrily, stumbling to his feet, "Better stop him…" And he shuffled out of the cave, leaving his rifle behind.

Like greased lightning, Thomas shook me

off, raced forward and picked up the gun. "Stay where you are, Pol! No point in letting them know there are two of us," he said over his shoulder. "Pick up a rock – get ready…"

The words were hardly out of his mouth before we heard the sound of someone scrabbling back up the rocks into the cave. It was the injured man. Blood was dripping down his face as Thomas shouted, "Stick your hands up!"

"What … what's goin' on…?" The man stared furiously at Thomas. "You little—!" he yelled, and jerked forward to wrench the gun from Thomas's hand, but Thomas pulled the trigger and a shot screamed through the air, exploding on the roof of the cave.

"Get back. Put your hands up … or I'll shoot again – I'll shoot again!" shouted Thomas.

The man backed away, his hands slowly rising into the air, swearing and cursing under his breath. Gripping a sharp rock I watched from the corner, rigid with fear.

The cave was set in the cliff-face, above the beach. On one side of the cave, the shingle-covered rocks sloped down to the beach, but the other was overlooking a sheer drop down to the sea where a channel ran under the cliff, and where the seals swam when the tide was high. Thomas slowly walked the man to the entrance overlooking the drop.

"Jump!" he ordered, pointing the gun at him.

The man looked down at the drop below. "Blimey! I can't swim, mate!" he whimpered.

"Jump!" Thomas shouted furiously. "Jump! I'll shoot if you don't!"

The man cowered away from the gun, shaking his head and moaning. "I daren't – I'm afraid of heights … I'm…" Suddenly I saw his expression change and his eyes widen as he saw something, behind Thomas. Then it all happened so fast.

"Behind you!" I screamed, and Thomas turned to see the shadow of the second man looming up, gun pointing. With a frantic effort Thomas lifted the rifle he was holding high above his head, and chucked it out of the cave, down into the sea. The first man yelled with fury, tried to catch the rifle, missed, staggered back and fell, screaming, into the water below.

The man with the gun lurched past Thomas with a grunt of astonishment.

"Quick, Pol!" shouted Thomas, grabbing my hand, and we raced out of the cave, sliding and slipping down the slope and across the beach. Then a shot rang out and a bullet whined past our heads – and then another. A large crop of rock suddenly appeared in front of us. We ducked behind it and crouched there, while more bullets whined above us and ricocheted against the rocks, like something out of the movies. I leaned against the rocks and closed my eyes. I felt I couldn't possibly be brave any more. I wanted to be back in the lighthouse, safe and sound, with Mum and Dad and Betty and Squawkette. Then I realized the bullets had stopped.

"What's going on?" Thomas mumbled. He began to ease up the rock.

"Tommo – keep down!" I screamed, and yanked him back.

"OK, you little brats!" a horrible voice snarled. "You've had it! This time I'm gonna get you!" We heard footsteps crunching towards us over the pebbles.

Suddenly I felt angry. This vile man had not only killed the baby seals, but now he was threatening to kill us!

Before Thomas knew what I was doing I jumped up and yelled, "Stop! The police are on their way. I phoned them. They'll be here soon!"

The man did stop, but he lifted his gun and pointed it at me.

"You'll get done for murder!" I shouted. "Don't be stupid! You can't get away. I've given them all the information about your ship – and – and stuff!" My voice was shaking. The man glared at me and lowered the gun. "Honestly!" My voice was getting hoarse with desperation. Thomas's head appeared above the rock and he stood up beside me.

"If you let us go, we'll say so – in court." He stopped and thought for a moment. "We'll say you stopped the other man from killing us – it'll get you off!" he invented quickly.

The man looked at us suspiciously. "Oh, yeah?" he snarled.

"Yes! We give you our word!" Thomas put his hand on his heart. "And we never lie!"

The man sneered, "Yer don't say!" He thought for a moment, a cunning look coming over his face. "But how come you're gonna tell a lie, then – in court – by sayin' I stopped me mate killin' you?"

"Well..." Thomas thought quickly. "It is the truth, isn't it? I mean – if you hadn't rushed out of the cave, your mate wouldn't have walked out after you and I wouldn't have got his gun and he wouldn't have fallen over the edge – and he would have killed us. Wouldn't he?"

The man, obviously not very bright, wrinkled his brow in thought, trying to follow Thomas's line of reasoning.

"The police will be here soon – any moment!" I pleaded.

The man looked nervously over his shoulder and then came to a decision. "OK, you kids. Come with me!" He pointed the gun at us again. "Walk! Go on! Up the beach!" We hadn't bargained for this. We'd thought he'd let us go, and while we hesitated, looking at

135

each other, he snarled, "Go on, or I *will* kill you! Move!"

"Where to?" panted Thomas as we began to half run, half walk, up the beach.

"The bloody castle!" roared the man, "And don't you put a foot wrong – or you'll get a bullet in your back!"

He shouted and snarled at us all the way up the beach, along the track and up the motte. Every now and then we'd turn and see him, red-faced, sweating and lumbering after us with his gun pointed menacingly at our backs. We didn't dare try anything. By the time we stumbled over the drawbridge and into the exercise yard, we were gasping for breath and so exhausted we could hardly see. Through and into the castle he directed us, across the main hall, pale and coldly beautiful with shafts of moonlight shining through the ruined walls.

"I know where he's taking us," whispered Thomas.

"Shut up!" growled the man, "Keep walkin'. Down there!" He pointed us down the narrow, winding staircase and we went, down, down, down into the depths of the castle.

"You know where you are now, don't ya?" the man sneered, as he fumbled in his pocket and brought out a key. We looked down at the huge, heavy grille on the floor. Underneath this were the dungeons, cold, dank and dark, the only part of the castle we'd never been able to explore. The grille had always been too heavy for us to lift up, and Dad had warned us not to try. It was too dangerous. If we fell in, we might break a leg. Now, we noticed with surprise, the grille had a large, new padlock on it. With one hand still pointing the rifle at us, the man put the key in the lock and opened it.

"You!" He pointed the gun at Thomas. "Take the padlock off and give it to me – and don't try anything funny!"

"Sorry, Polly," sighed Thomas as he did as he was told.

"Now," said the man, pocketing the padlock, "lift up the grille. Go on – you can manage it – both of you!"

We were aching with tiredness, but we bent down and tried to lift the grille. It was incredibly heavy. We began to prise it up slowly, pushing with all our might.

"Ah – you useless little—!" With a snarl, the man stuck the heel of his boot under the grille and threw it up. "Now. Jump!" he ordered. We stood at the edge of the black, evil hole, just looking at him. "Go on – what are you waitin' for?"

"But no one will ever find us," Thomas whispered.

"Shut up!" the man roared. "This is it! If you don't jump, I'll send a bullet to help you!"

And so we jumped. Thomas first and then me.

Seconds after we had landed on the cold floor, we heard the sound of the grille overhead slamming shut and the rattle of the padlock being secured, followed by the footsteps of the man becoming fainter and fainter as he ran up the stairs.

CHAPTER FIFTEEN

It was a few moments before either of us spoke.

"Tommo ... are you all right?" My voice sounded feeble and shaky. I couldn't see him, but he must have been quite close because I could hear him whisper.

"Yes." Then he gave a huge sigh. "Ohhh. We don't have to whisper now, Pol," he said, really softly and sadly, as if it was the end of the world.

"Oh ... no ... I mean, yes..." I whispered. He was right, of course, but my voice had sort of shrivelled up and wouldn't come out right. Lying on the cold stone floor, deep under the castle, far away from home or warmth or food or Mum and Dad or Betty or Squawkette or stars or moon or sunlight or wind, I'd never felt more hopeless in my life.

"What are we going to do?" I said, and my

voice was tiny.

"Oh … Pol." Thomas's voice sounded miles away. He put his arms around me. "Just try and keep warm," he whispered. Then he spoke loudly. "We've got to be brave, Pol. There's no one here but us…"

"There's us!" said a strong voice nearby – a voice we knew well.

"Dad?" we whimpered, with shock and disbelief. Then we both yelled together, "Dad – Dad – Dad!"

"And your mother," he said, coming closer. "She's asleep now…"

"No I'm not!" said the other voice we knew so well. It was so dark we couldn't see anything. But in a minute we were all hugging one another, laughing and crying at the same time. The darkness and the cold were so much more bearable now.

We hardly needed to be told what had happened to Mum and Dad. We'd already guessed that they had been pounced on by the seal hunters and dragged up here and thrown in the dungeon, but Mum and Dad were gobsmacked at *our* story. We just kept telling it over and over.

"You should have seen Betty attack the hunter – she was so brave!" said Thomas. "And the scratches on his face…"

"You should have seen Tommo with the gun," I said. "He was amazing. He shot at the roof – just like in a film. You should have heard the noise!"

"But it was Polly's idea in the first place," said Thomas. "She was the one who insisted on coming. We could have waited for help to arrive, but she insisted..."

"Help is arriving, by the way," I interrupted. "Tommo thought of that."

"I contacted HQ before we left. They said they'd send a ship straight away. It shouldn't be long."

"It'll be some hours from your call," said Dad slowly. "I wonder why they didn't say they'd send a helicopter?"

"Well, we didn't know exactly what was happening. When I contacted HQ, I only told them about the seal slaughter, and that you and Mum hadn't returned. But you said you'd be gone until at least midnight, and it was only just a quarter past," said Thomas regretfully.

"Well, never mind. They'll be here sometime," said Mum soothingly.

"But ... but ... will they find us down here?" I said, wishing like mad I didn't have to ask that question.

"Darling – they'll search the whole island. When they find we're not in the lighthouse, they'll look everywhere. We'll just have to listen out for them and then make sure when they get to the castle that we all make a huge noise, so they know we're down here," Mum said reassuringly. But I wasn't convinced.

We all agreed that Betty was sure to be safe. "I think I saw her hiding in the bushes above the beach while we were running along," said Thomas. "I didn't call out, of course. She'll be all right. She didn't get shot, anyway."

"Don't suppose you managed to bring any food?" said Dad.

"I had a whole backpack full of food," I said. "But I had to leave it at the top of the cliffs. I'd never have got down the tunnel with it on." And then suddenly I remembered something. I dug in my pocket and pulled out the large chocolate bar. "I'd forgotten about this – look!"

"Polly – you angel!" said Mum. "We've had nothing since, since…"

"About lunch-time!" Dad interrupted, "But it feels like a week or more. Come on, pass it round!"

It was rather battered and slightly soft from being in my coat for so long, but it tasted wonderful.

"Mustn't eat it all, though," said Mum. "Just in case…" She didn't want to say "just in case we don't get out soon," but we all knew what she meant.

We huddled together on the cold floor, trying not to lean against the damp walls because that made us even colder. But we were so tired that in the end we just sort of collapsed.

"How many other poor prisoners have sat here, in the past?" was the last thing I thought, as I cuddled up to Mum. Then, despite the cold and the hard floor, we fell asleep.

At one time I woke up and heard footsteps pacing the dungeon from wall to wall. It was Dad. He told us later that he had been so worried that we couldn't survive long in that place without food or water, and that he had thought that the chances of us being found were pretty slim. But when I whispered his name he sat down beside me, gave me a hug and told me to go to sleep again – that help would be there soon. And I believed him, and felt safe, and went back to sleep.

When I woke up again, the palest light of dawn was filtering into the dungeon. Then I began to be really frightened. We'd been there all night. No one had rescued us yet! Would they ever come?

Everyone else was still asleep. I wanted to hear them say, "Don't worry, Polly. It will be all right," but instead it was just me huddled on the floor with my head on my arms, trying to be brave and wait for them to wake up.

I was beginning to feel desperate when I heard a small "Miaow?", a sort of question-type miaow. At first I hardly noticed it. And then from the grille above came a louder "Miaow?" I jumped up and stood underneath it.

"Betty?" I called softly, not wanting to

wake Mum and Dad and Tommo just in case I was imagining it. "Is that you, Betty?"

"Miaow – miaow – aohw!" said the voice. Betty's little nose sniffed through the grille and her big eyes stared down. I stood on tiptoes and could just reach my fingers up high enough for her to lick them.

"Hullo, Betty – hullo, hullo!" I said. "You've found us! You clever, clever cat!" She purred and licked my fingers. "Now you know where we are, perhaps you'll lead the rescuers here? Betty, Betty." I called her name gently and lovingly as she stared down, licking my fingertips again and again.

I heard someone behind me stir and stand up. Dad staggered over, rubbing his back and looking anxious. When he saw Betty's nose poking through the grille, he grinned.

"She's found us, Dad – she's found us!" I kept saying. "I bet she'll lead the search party to us – I bet she will!"

"Shhh!" He nodded and pointed to the other two, still asleep, but they both stirred at the sound of our whispering.

"Betty!" Thomas shouted and got up as quickly as he could. We stood looking up at her, calling her name over and over, while she mewed and looked pleased and tried to get to us. She probably couldn't understand why we didn't open the grille to let her in, and after a while she sat looking quite mournful. Then she ran away and came back soon after, dropping a small mouse through the grille onto my upturned face.

I squealed and shuddered and laughed at the same time. "She's trying to feed us. Oh, Betty – you're such a good girl!"

"Go and get help, Betty. Bring them to us!" Thomas called, but we all knew there was no point until help actually arrived. Betty sat on top of the grille for a while, obviously puzzled that we wouldn't let her in, and then disappeared.

"Let's eat the rest of the chocolate," said Mum, unwrapping what was now a very yukky-looking mess. There was enough for each of us to have a couple of pieces, but not enough to take the edge off our hunger.

It was so cold. We sat glumly huddled together and could hardly get our minds off the cold. Finally Thomas said, "Who knows a joke?" but nobody could think of one.

"OK, tell us a poem then, Mum," said Thomas.

Now I thought about all the times she'd said, "It's a pity they don't teach children to learn poems by heart any more – such useful furniture for the brain!" I wished my brain was fully furnished with lots of poems that I could think of, just to take my mind off where my body was. "A funny one," I said, "The one about Jim being eaten by the lion."

Mum had just got to the part which goes:

"Now just imagine how it feels
When first your toes and then your heels,
And then by gradual degrees,
Your shins and ankles, calves and knees,
Are slowly eaten, bit by bit,
No wonder Jim detested it!"

when she stopped suddenly and listened, and
we all heard footsteps, faintly at first, then
louder, and a voice saying something we
couldn't make out. We looked at each other
warily. It could be help – or it could be the
hunters, coming back. We sat absolutely still,
eyes turned upwards to the grille. And then a
face appeared. Jeremy's!

It was obvious that at first he couldn't see a
thing. It was too dark, and coming from outside – his eyes not being used to the darkness
– all he could see was a black hole. Then he
saw us, and as he said later we were just a
small bunch of frightened faces, looking up at
him.

"Good Lord!" he said loudly "It's you!
Wow! You're all here – and alive! What
incredible luck!"

"Jeremy!" Dad stood up and went over
to the grille. "Who ... sent you?" he asked
carefully.

Jeremy's face broke into a grin. "Not the

enemy, buddy!" He put his hand through the grille and Dad reached up.

"What!" Dad was astounded. "You don't mean...?"

"HQ sent me."

We all scrambled to our feet and came over to the grille, reaching our hands up and trying to touch him, Tommo and I jumping up and down and shouting his name over and over.

"Shhh! Quiet, everyone!" said Dad. "Jeremy – get us out of here as fast as you can, will you. Please – hurry – hurry!" he begged.

"OK. Hang loose. Got to get reinforce-mements. Back in a flash!" Jeremy yelled, and rushed off.

Mum stood looking up at the small patch of slatted light coming from the grille. "I hope it's not a false alarm," she said.

Dad put his arms around her. "It's all right now, Yassie, it's all right."

"Oh, Dylan – I hope so. But maybe it's a trick?" she murmured.

I knew it would be OK. "It won't be a false alarm – you'll see!" I said, remembering why I was so sure. "We knew last night that Jeremy didn't throw Betty in the lake – didn't we, Tommo? Remember? Those men said they did it. Jeremy's been OK, right from the start."

"Well – he could have still been working with them," said Thomas, guardedly. "But I don't think he is."

Very quickly Jeremy was back, with two other men. "Stand away from the grille. We're going to have to bash the padlock off!" he called, and they began banging it. Within minutes the lock was broken, the grille was up and Jeremy had jumped down into the dungeon.

"Hi there, little Polly Pickford!" he said, giving me an enormous hug. "Didn't think you'd be seeing me again so soon, did you? Hi, Thomas. Great to see you – really great!"

"How did you find us here?" I asked, when everyone had said hello and fantastic to see you, and all that stuff. Suddenly a small face appeared at the top of the grille and with a squeak of impatience a little furry body hurled itself down into my arms.

"That's how!" said Jeremy, laughing. "That darned cat! The moment we landed she wouldn't leave me alone until I followed her here. HQ sent a ship, but I came by helicopter. Realized something was wrong when I tried to contact you after HQ got that message. I persuaded them to send me back real quick … oh, the ship has already picked up the seal hunter. He's safely stowed in the hold – in irons, as he should be! Now, come on Polly – you can be the first out to freedom."

He picked me up, with Betty still clinging on, and pushed me through the open grille to where another large man pulled me the rest of the way.

*   *   *

It wasn't until much later that day – after we'd all had food and hot baths and talked to Squawkette and slept for a while and showed Jeremy all over the lighthouse – that we sat down and really talked to him.

"Yes, I knew you were suspicious of me," he admitted. "But don't forget, I was suspicious of you too. Didn't know who you were, or what you were doing here. But I wondered about your story of wanting a nice quiet place to bring up the kids. Thought the most likely scenario was that you were working for the enemy – been set up by one of the big organizations to pass on info to smugglers and pirate ships. And you must admit, you kids behaved quite … um … strangely, at times!"

"Oh, wasn't it terrible!" I groaned at the thought of it. "All that pretending – that we didn't care much about the baby seals."

"And you were spying on me at the castle, weren't you, Thomas!"

"Of course I was," Thomas said sternly. "I wasn't taking any chances!"

"But what were you doing sailing around our island?" Mum asked. "It really looked as if you had been sent by some enemy organization to spy on us!"

"That," said Jeremy with a grin, "was pure fate. Funny thing, fate! I just happened to be on holiday. And my idea of a holiday is not

149

lying on a beach in the sun for days on end. I'm one of those mad yachtsmen. One day I plan to sail around the world, single-handed. In the meantime, every moment I get I spend sailing in my little yacht ... which is now at the bottom of the sea. But thanks to you all, *I'll* live to sail another day!"

"Well, I don't suppose we'd have believed you if you'd told us that at the time. But I'm extremely glad it's all true," said Dad.

"Wasn't until I got back to HQ that I found out all about you. Too late *then* to tell you that we're on the same side! But I'd thought I might send you a Christmas card," said Jeremy chuckling.

Betty jumped up on his knee and lifted her little nose up for a kiss. "Angowh, angowh!" she said.

"Maybe a Christmas hamper would be more in order," he said, hugging her. "Lots of turkey and smoked salmon and honey-roast ham, eh?" Betty purred and purred.

"Ark, ark, ark!" screeched a cross voice from the corner.

"Not forgetting a large sack of luxury parrot food!"

"Poor old Squawkette." Thomas went over to the cage and stroked her gently through the bars. "I know you've been feeling left out – but you don't know how lucky you are!"

"Maybe she's not so lucky," I said. "Now

150

we know what it feels like to be in a cage. I can see her point of view."

"I think she's been making good use of her time behind bars practising a whole lot of new insults for – guess who?" said Mum, holding Betty up to the cage.

Squawkette's head spun round and she glared at the cat, and bobbing her bandaged body up and down like an animated Egyptian mummy, she croaked, "Bossy Betty – grossy Betty, grotty Betty, greedy Betty – I'll getcha, Betty – I'll getcha – I'll getcha!"

Tommo and I groaned. There was going to be big trouble when she got out.

BECAUSE OF WINN-DIXIE
Kate DiCamillo

One summer's day, ten-year-old India Opal Buloni goes down to the local supermarket for some groceries – and comes home with a dog.

Winn-Dixie is no ordinary dog. Big, skinny and smelly he may be, but he also has the most winning smile. It's because of Winn-Dixie that Opal gets to know some very surprising people and starts to make new friends. It's because of Winn-Dixie that she finally dares to ask her father about her mother, who left when Opal was three. In fact, just about everything that happens that summer is because of Winn-Dixie.

Read about the exploits of this most unusual dog and a host of quirky characters in this enchanting tale.

THE STRANGE CHANGE
OF FLORA YOUNG
Nick Warburton

Would *you* like to be a grown-up for the day?

Quiet, shy Flora Young is alarmed when her teacher, Mrs Camp, announces that she wants to give Flora a part in the school play. Especially since she'll have to wear a dirty old mask found at the back of the stock cupboard. But when Flora tries the mask on, she discovers it makes her feel different – assertive and in charge. And it soon becomes clear that it's having the reverse effect on Mrs Camp!

How can Flora make the most of her new-found confidence while it lasts? Find out in this exciting and humorous story by award-winning author Nick Warburton.

LOVE, RUBY LAVENDER
Deborah Wiles

Poor Ruby Lavender! Her fellow chicken-lover, best friend and grandmother, Miss Eula Dapplevine, has upped and left town on an open ticket to Hawaii to visit her new baby granddaughter – and it looks like it's going to be a long, empty summer for Ruby.

But as it turns out, she finds plenty to write about. In letter after letter Ruby tells her grandmother of the exciting developments in the chicken house, her new friend Dove and her old enemy Melba Jane, the bane of her life. But there's one thing Ruby won't talk about to anyone – not Miss Eula, nor Dove, nor her mother – and it's the very same thing that makes her take the long way home every day...

Meet the enchanting Ruby Lavender. She's funny, she's feisty, she'll tug at your heart!

THE DREAM DOG
Enid Richemont

Josh wants a dog. He wasn't allowed one in the flat, but now his family has moved to a house with a proper garden, surely a dog would be fine here? Then, the very first night, something amazing happens – a dog appears at Josh's bedside, a funny-looking mongrel with a silly grin. But it's not real, Josh can't stroke it; it's a sort of dream dog. Is it a ghost? Is Josh imagining it? Or could it – in some mysterious way – be real after all?

Readers will be touched and intrigued by this double story, seen through the eyes of both Josh and the "dream" dog.